QUEEN OF FIRST DATES

JAIMIE CASE

DEDICATED

To all the women that still believe in true love.

BLURB

30 dates in 30 days. Seems like fun right? Yeah, not so much...

When my boss asked me to write an article about online dating and more specifically the do's and don'ts of first dates, I expected it to be a mess. I hadn't expected it to be a complete and utter disaster, though. How was I to know that I'd be paired up with arrogant, cocky, and "too handsome for his own good," Nolan Montgomery.

Nolan had always treated me as his little sister's annoying best friend and I couldn't stand his bossy ways. The last thing I needed was him following me around with a video camera and lecturing me on all the things I was doing wrong. I certainly didn't need him showing me how I could improve; even if his lips and hands were recurring images in my dreams. He may have been my first kiss, but there was no way I was going to let him get his hands on me again.

PROLOGUE

Ten Years Ago

"Romeo, Romeo, wherefore art thou, Romeo?" The words tripped off of my lips in a scared fashion and I looked over at Betsy to see her reaction.

"Not bad," she said, giving me an eager smile. "You're a really good actress, Jules."

"No, I'm not." I shook my head and sunk onto the floor and leaned back against her bedroom door. "I don't know how I got this part..." My voice trailed off as I thought about the part that most worried me.

"What's wrong?" Betsy asked me, her curly blond hair framing her face in a totally cute way. A way that made me so jealous because my straight dark brown hair never hung around my face in a cute way.

"Nothing," I mumbled and looked down.

"Don't lie to me, Jules," she said, jumping off of her bed and walking toward me. "Tell me what's wrong?"

"Nothing." I shook my head as she sat next to me on the ground, her red cheerleading skirt riding up slightly.

"Julia Gilbert, tell me what's wrong."

"I don't know how to kiss," I whined as I waited for her to laugh at me, but she didn't laugh. She just looked at me with a supportive smile.

"Do you want me to give you some pointers?" she asked helpfully.

"Can we get some ice cream first?" I offered her a quick smile and she just laughed.

"Come on, then." She jumped up and grabbed my arm and pulled me up. "I don't know what flavors we have though. Grandma Elsie did the shopping this week because my folks are in England on a second honeymoon and she just doesn't get the need for good ice cream flavors."

"That's okay, any ice cream is okay." I laughed as we walked out of her bedroom and headed toward the kitchen. I could hear loud rock music blasting from her brother Nolan's room as we walked by it. "How's Nolan?" I asked her lightly, as if I didn't care that he hadn't joined us at dinner because he'd had to stay late for a baseball game.

"As annoying as ever." She rolled her eyes as we made it to the kitchen and she opened the freezer. "You would think he's the only guy that's ever been a senior in high school, with a freshman sister. I'm ruining his life and all that good stuff. Okay, we have two different types to choose from." She held up two tubs of ice cream. One was plain vanilla, and the other was plain strawberry.

"No, dulce de leche?" I asked hopefully, and she laughed as she shook her head.

"Vanilla or strawberry?" she asked me as she cocked her head to the side. "I think we have some whipped cream though, so we can add some of that to the top."

"Whipped cream?" Nolan's voice sounded from behind me and I turned around and gave him a huge grin.

"Hi, Nolan."

"Hi, nerd," he said as he walked past me and rubbed the top of my head. "How you doing?"

"Not bad," I said, my heart racing as I stared at him. He was still in his Canyon Beach varsity baseball team uniform and he looked hotter than ever. His dark hair was close to the top of his head and his blue eyes sparkled as he studied my face. "I'm staying over tonight. Betsy is helping me learn lines."

"Jules got the lead in the school play," Betsy said proudly. "She's awesome."

"I'm not awesome." I shook my head. "I think I impressed Mr. Duncan because I knew all the lines but that's only because I love Shakespeare. I've read all of his plays."

"That's because you and Stella are book nerds." Betsy laughed as she mentioned my younger cousin. It was true, of course. Betsy and I both loved books and had spent many sleepovers discussing our favorite authors and novels. However, just because I loved Shakespeare's writing didn't mean I was a good actress. I knew Betsy was trying to be nice because she was my best friend, but I knew my acting ability was mediocre at best.

"So you're Juliet?" Nolan's eyes lit up as he looked me up and down. "I can see that."

"Thank you," I said, even though what he said couldn't really be construed as a compliment.

"I'll be at the shows taking photos of the cast at the opening." Nolan grinned before he turned around and opened the fridge and pulled out a carton of milk. Nolan was the school photographer. He took photos for the school paper and the yearbook and everybody could see how talented he was. He wanted to attend photography school, but his parents had said no way, so instead, he was going to school in New York City, at NYU, in fact, and I was positive I was going to miss him more than anything. Nolan was the perfect guy. He was handsome, sporty, and artistic. It was a pity that he had no idea that I existed. Well, he knew I existed as Betsy's best friend. But he didn't see me as a woman. Unfortunately.

"That's so cool," I said to his back as Betsy started scooping out ice cream. "Will you stay to watch the play?"

"Of course." He turned around and gave me a boyish grin. "I wouldn't want to miss that."

"If Jules can work up the courage to kiss Romeo that is." Betsy laughed and I could feel my face growing red.

"Betsy!" I chided her for letting out my secret.

"Oh, oops." She wrinkled her nose and then rolled her eyes. "It's only Nolan, and he doesn't care."

"Care about what?" Nolan asked curiously, his eyes staring at me with interest.

"Jules has to kiss Romeo, and she's nervous because she's never kissed anyone before and..." Her voice trailed off as I gave her a death stare. "Maybe I do have a big mouth..." She shook her head, and I watched as her blond curls bounced as I sighed slightly. "Sorry, Jules, I suck."

"You've never kissed a guy before?" Nolan walked over to me and stopped directly in front of me. "That surprises me," he said, his green eyes twinkling. I stared into his eyes, unable to breathe. He was just so handsome. It always surprised me that Nolan had green eyes and Betsy had blue. I thought as siblings they'd have the same color eyes and hair, but they are totally different. You wouldn't even know they were siblings from afar, but from up close you could see they had the same nose, the same teeth, and the same widespread smile that made you feel like a million dollars when it was directed at you.

"Don't tease her, Nolan. We all can't be horndogs like

you," Betsy teased her brother, and I blushed at her use of the word *horndog*.

"Do you kiss a lot of girls then?" I asked him innocently, not sure I wanted to know the answer.

"I do." He grinned. "I'm a bit of a kissing expert. Do you need some help?" He winked at me and I could feel my face heating up. I couldn't believe he'd asked me that. Did he mean it or was he just teasing me?

"What would your girlfriend say?" I asked wondering if he was dating Britney, the head cheerleader on Betsy's squad.

"I don't have a girlfriend. Why tie myself down?" He laughed as he opened the cupboard and took out a bag of Oreo's. "Anyway, I'm going back to playing Xbox, have a good night, nerds."

"You're a nerd," Betsy said, but she laughed when he rubbed the top of her head. "Brothers," she said as she rolled her eyes and handed me a bowl of ice cream. "Ready to go back and continue practicing?"

"Let's do it," I said as I grabbed a spoon and followed her down the corridor and back to her room. I could hear her mumbling something as we walked, but all I could think about was what Nolan had said when he'd offered me some kissing help. Did he like me then? Did he really want to kiss me? What did it mean? My brain was about to blow up with questions, but I didn't want to ask Betsy what she thought. For some reason, I was embarrassed for her to find out I had a small crush on her brother.

BETSY HAD FALLEN INTO AN ICE CREAM COMA ABOUT AN hour after we'd gotten back to her room and was snoring on her bed. I looked down at the script in my hands and bit down on my lower lip. Everything seemed so much more insurmountable when Betsy wasn't awake to boost my spirits. I picked up the ice cream bowls and walked them to the kitchen before going to brush my teeth. I placed them in the sink to rinse out before placing them in the dishwasher.

"Oh, dearie, there's no need to do the dishes." Betsy's grandma Elsie rubbed my shoulder as she came up behind me with a slight yawn.

"Oh, it's okay. I don't want them to dry out," I said with a small smile.

"You're a good girl," she said, her blue eyes shining tenderly at me. "How have you been, Julia?"

"Good, Grandma Elsie. I'm just learning my lines for the school play." I made a face. "It's hard."

"Oh, I do remember loving acting when I was a little girl. I was a natural." She turned the kettle on and smiled to herself. "Though, if I'm honest, I was a better dancer than an actress. I just loved the Vienna waltz."

"Oh yeah?" I asked. I had no idea what the Vienna waltz was.

"And the tango." She smiled. "Betsy's grandad was a good dancer. We took ballroom classes when we were younger."

"Oh, I didn't know that." I smiled at her. "That's cool."

"So let me hear some of your lines then, dear."

"Oh?" I made a face. "I don't know many off the top of my head."

"Well, let me hear what you know." She gave me a loving smile and so I cleared my throat and started to recite the lines I could remember.

"O Romeo, Romeo, wherefore art thou Romeo?

Deny thy father and refuse thy name;

Or, if thou wilt not, be but sworn my love,

And I'll no longer be a Capulet." I stopped then because I could feel someone behind me. I turned around slowly and lo and behold, there stood Nolan.

"Lady, by yonder blessed moon I vow,

That tips with silver all these fruit-tree tops—" he said with a grin and I heard Grandma Elsie clapping.

"That's not the next line," I said as I gazed at him in a daze. He could quote Shakespeare?

"Well, you would know better than me," he said. "You sounded good, nerd."

"Oh, thank you." I smiled at him, grateful in the knowledge that I hadn't known that he'd been listening when I'd started.

"Now, you two are so sweet," Grandma Elsie said, and I looked over at her. She was still beaming and nodding her head slightly. "Well, I'm off to bed now. I'll see you both in the morning. Blueberry pancakes sound good?"

"Yummy." I nodded.

"They sound good, but I'm sure Betsy's going to add some weird ingredient to them." Nolan groaned. "She always experiments with food."

"Your sister is a good cook, Nolan," Grandma Elsie said. "You're lucky she loves to cook for you so much."

"I'm so lucky." He rolled his eyes, but I knew that he appreciated her food. "Night, Gran." There was silence for a few seconds as Grandma Elsie headed off to bed and then he cleared his throat. "So," he said and he was grinning.

"So what?" I asked him confused.

"You're up late."

"Was just returning the bowls."

"Uh-huh." He had a knowing look on his face. "So, want to take me up on my offer?"

"What offer?" I said and then my jaw dropped as I realized what he was saying. "You want to kiss me?"

"You're a little kid, I don't want to kiss you. I want to teach you how not to mess up your scene."

"I'm not a little kid. We're both in high school."

"You're a freshman and I'm a senior." He gave me a haughty look. "In my eyes, you're a kid."

"Because you're so old and mature."

"Feisty," he said with a little laugh as he stepped closer to me. "Your eyes spark little brown daggers at me when you're angry."

"I'm not angry," I said and blushed as he grabbed my hand. "What are you doing?" I swallowed hard.

"Holding your hand." He smiled and then he leaned forward, his eyes staring into mine the whole time and he kissed me, his lips pressed against mine for a few seconds before I started kissing him back. I could see his eyes widen as I pushed my tongue into his mouth. In all the movies I'd seen, a kiss didn't mean anything if there wasn't tongue involved. Then he reached his hand to the back of my head and cradled my neck as he kissed me back and I melted against him. My whole body was on fire and I could feel butterflies in my stomach. When he moved back a minute later, I felt like I was flying. I smiled at him shyly, wondering if he had felt the same thing I had. His expression was confused as he gazed at me, his eyes on my lips for a few seconds.

"Wow," I said with a bright smile. "Just wow." He looked down at my pajamas and I groaned inwardly as I realized I was wearing the Frozen pajamas my parents had gotten me for Christmas because they still thought I was a little kid.

"Not bad. Keep practicing, nerd." And then he rubbed the top of my head. "Keep reading those Jane Austen books you love and you'll be okay. See ya." He then headed back to his room as I continued standing there in the middle of the hallway watching after him, feeling embarrassed. It was only when he got to his bedroom door, that he turned around and looked at me again. He stared at me for a few seconds and I wondered what he was thinking. He gave me a small wave and entered his room. I wanted to run to his room and beg him to kiss me again, but I didn't. Instead, I just stood there and rubbed my lips softly. I'd just had my first ever kiss, and it had been amazing. Absolutely amazing. Nolan Montgomery was the most popular guy at Canyon Beach High School and my best friend's brother and I didn't know if it would ever happen again. I only hoped that in some universe he would somehow turn into my Prince Charming because I needed to experience another kiss like that again in my life.

❧ I ❧

PRESENT DAY

"It's the thing now, Jules. Everyone is meeting their partners on online dating services. That's how they get all these dates." My boss, Malcolm Jones stared at me over the top of his glasses. "I want you to write a weekly article on the do's and don'ts of first dates."

"But I'm not on any online dating sites," I said weakly, hoping he would accept that as an excuse as to why I shouldn't have to write this particular article series. "Can't you ask Susan?"

"Susan is covering the current crisis in Syria." Malcolm shook his head impatiently and then pointed his pen at me. "You're the perfect person for the job."

"Great," I said and held in a sigh. No point in acting like a petulant little kid. At least not in front of Malcolm. He couldn't care less that I hated going on first dates and I certainly wasn't going to tell him that I was one of the people that needed to read the article I was supposed to write. I'll have to save my moaning for later when I'm having dinner with my best friend, Betsy. She knows all the woes that make up my crappy dating life.

"We'll have a photographer following you around as well." He's scribbling notes furiously as he completely ignored the stressed-out look on my face.

"A photographer?" I stared at my boss and didn't bother to hide the disdain and horror on my face. "What do you mean a photographer?" Did I really need a witness to the suckage that was my personality on a first date? I didn't want anyone to see how badly I embarrassed myself. Canyon Beach was a small town, and I didn't need to be the talk of people's dinner conversations.

"You went to college, Julia. I mean a man with a camera." He beamed at me. "He'll be taking videos and photos. So you'll be all mic'd up, just like you asked for."

"When did I ask to be connected to a microphone?" My eyes narrowed. "I never asked for that."

"Last week, did you or did you not come into my office and ask to be an investigative reporter?"

"You what?" My jaw dropped as I stared at him in shock. This asshole didn't seriously equate me wanting to be an investigative reporter with me being followed on awful dates around the city, did he?

"I recall the conversation quite vividly," he continued, and I held up my hand, trying not to cuss him out.

"Malcolm, do you really think me going on some cheap dates with a bunch of loser guys and being followed by some wannabe cameraman is the same thing as me going under-cover in the Middle East and trying to figure out world peace?"

"Do you really think you can figure out world peace when you can't even decide what type of sandwich you want at lunchtime?" he said with a sarcastic tone that I chose to ignore. He knew me too well.

"I'm not even going to dignify that comment with a response." I put my nose up in the air and avoided his gaze.

"Good, good." He nodded, barely paying attention to me. Sometimes he reminded me of my dad in the way his eyes would glaze over when my mom and I talked about shopping or my nonexistent love life. "Now, Nolan will be here in the next few minutes and we'll be able to continue discussing the plans then."

"Nolan?" I said slowly, my entire body going stiff as I blinked rapidly at him. "Not Nolan Montgomery?" Please, dear God, don't let him be talking about Nolan Montgomery! Though I knew the answer before he responded. How many photographers named Nolan lived in Canyon Beach? I could only think of one.

"Yes, Nolan Montgomery." He smiled at me. "Oh yes, he's Betsy's brother, isn't he?"

"Uh-huh," I mumbled, trying not to panic. I wanted to jump up and run out of the office. I didn't want to see Nolan Montgomery, let alone work with him.

"Then that's even better." He nodded and tapped the files on his desk. "Perfect, just perfect." He stared and all I could do was stifle a groan. I couldn't stand Nolan Montgomery. He had been the bane of my existence for most of my life. He was the older brother of my best friend Betsy and he had always acted like he was the boss of both of us. Not to mention the rest of my history with him. I didn't even want to think about certain events.

"What's perfect?" A familiar deep husky voice sounded from behind me. I didn't have to turn around to know that it was Nolan. I'd know his voice in my dreams. That was the problem with living in a small town like Canyon Beach, everyone knew everyone, and you couldn't escape the people you never wanted to see. Especially, if they were the best photographer in town. Especially, if they were your best friend's brother. And he was your first kiss and more.

"I was just telling, Julia here, how perfect it is that her

best friend's brother was going to be the photographer she worked on with this story. This way you can get into the nitty-gritty, the deep and dirty without any holdups." Malcolm grinned widely, and I just stared at him with my mouth ajar. Was he for real? "Julia, you can feel free to truly be yourself on these dates and let Nolan capture the real you. It will be perfect for our weekly videos."

"What weekly videos?" Now my jaw was open wide and I could feel myself starting to sweat. "You didn't say anything about videos."

"Well, well, well." Malcolm just beamed at me. "Why don't you have a seat, Nolan?" He pointed to the chair that was way too close to me and I watched as Nolan squeezed past me to sit down. He grinned at me as he sat, giving me a quick wink before he looked back at Malcolm, a devious and humorous glint in his fern-green eyes.

"What weekly videos, Malcolm?" I said again, this time more sternly, my tone made of steel. I knew I needed to watch myself, after all, Malcolm was still my boss, but I was beside myself with annoyance. This was the last thing I needed. I squirmed in my seat just imagining Nolan watching and studying me on dates. It was embarrassing, plain and simple. I couldn't stand him. He was a boorish, rude, chauvinistic brute. I conveniently disregarded the fact that I'd had a not so secret crush on him when I'd first started high school. And the fact that he was my first official kiss was burned from my memory. I'd grown up since then. I wasn't even going to think about that night senior year or that moment when I was a sophomore in college. My face burned red as I stared at his familiar face. I almost felt like I was back in college.

"He's talking about the weekly 'Queen of First Dates,' video segment that will be on the *Canyon Beach Chronicle* website." Nolan turned to me with an infuriating know-it-all smirk. "I'm sure you know that more and more readers prefer to read their news online."

"Me going on dates isn't news." I glared at him, my heart thudding, ever so slightly.

"It sure is." He smiled widely, his eyes dancing in merriment. "When's the last time you've gone on a date, Jules? It will be the talk of the town."

"I don't want to be the talk of the town." My eyes narrowed as I stared at him. "And I go on plenty of dates, thank you very much."

"Uh-huh." He grinned as if he knew I was lying and then turned back to Malcolm. "I think it's a great idea. I was thinking about the turnaround time and I think I can have the videos edited in a few days, so if Jules keeps her first dates to a Friday or Saturday night, I can have the video edited and uploaded by Tuesday?"

"That's perfect." Malcolm looked like the cat that had swallowed the canary. And a big canary at that. I couldn't believe that the two of them were talking about this as if I were okay with it.

"I'm really not cool with this, Malcolm, it's invasive and personal... and..." I could see out of the corner of my eyes that Nolan was laughing at me and I turned to him with a death stare. "What are you laughing at?" I growled, wanting to hit him in the shoulder to get him to stop, but quickly remembered that I was no longer ten years old. I couldn't get away with just thumping him to stop him from teasing or tormenting me.

"I just find it funny that you're worried about something being too personal. You could have fooled me."

"What?"

"All the conversations you and Betsy have had regarding boys..." His voice trailed off and he raised an eyebrow at me. "Do you want me to continue?"

"Nolan Montgomery, you are the most infuriating man I have ever met." I folded my arms, gave him one last glare and turned back to Malcolm. "This is absolutely ridiculous! I don't think this is a good idea, at all." I stressed the last part and gave Malcolm my most professional look, while subliminally trying to tell him, *do what I say*.

"I'm sorry you feel that way, Julia." He gave me a sad look. "Unfortunately, circulation is down and we need for this to be a hit to get advertisers back on board." He let out a huge sigh. "I think we might have to close down if we don't increase our revenues soon."

"Humph." I just sat there with a burning face staring at him. I couldn't believe that he was going to pull the emotional manipulation trick on me. My videos on dating were not going to save the newspaper from going down. I pursed my lips as I looked at Malcolm's serious face and Nolan's half-laughing expression. "I guess I will try it out, under duress, to see if it will help raise advertising revenues, but I doubt it."

"Actually, we already have several businesses lining up to sponsor some of the dates," Malcolm said with a huge grin. "Tony's Pizzeria, Lottie's Flower Shop..." His voice trailed off as my expression turned steely again.

"Just how long have you been planning this column, Malcolm?" My voice was soft, and I knew from the way his eyes widened that he knew that I was this close to losing it.

"Jules, does it really matter?" Nolan answered for Malcolm in his typical alpha male fashion. "I would think that you'd be happy to get the chance to finally go on a bunch of dates. Heaven knows that you and Betsy have spent most of your lives talking about dating."

"Nolan Montgomery," I said his name sharply, fire spitting from my eyes as I looked upon his handsome face. His dark hair was cut short and I could tell from his light stubble that he hadn't shaved this morning. I wondered what he'd been doing last night that he didn't have time to shave this morning. I shook my head slightly to stop myself from going down that road. I really didn't care. At all. Nolan Montgomery was nothing to me.

"Yes, Julia Gilbert?" he drawled and smiled his lazy, you don't want to mess with me smile. I grabbed my phone and muttered under my breath.

"Just wait until I tell Betsy about this."

"See, it's like I said, nothing is too invasive for you. Just imagine I'm my sister when I'm following you around."

I didn't bother looking back at him then because I knew he would have a smug look on his face and I knew that I would want to wipe it off in any way possible. And I didn't want to get fired for assault and battery. And there was no way I wanted the police called because it was likely to be Jefferson Evian that showed up and he was Nolan's best friend. That was another problem living in a small town. The authorities were friends with your enemies. There was no way that Jefferson would understand where I was coming from if I slapped the daylights out of Nolan.

"Is there anything else you want to discuss, Malcolm?" I said finally, knowing there was nothing more to say. He wasn't going to change his mind. I just had to deal with it and come up with a plan.

"Well, there was one thing," he said and stuttered slightly. "Nolan, I know you said you would prefer the dates to be Friday's and Saturday's, but I had a different plan."

"Oh?" Nolan said surprised, and I hid a smile. *Yeah, Nolan, he's not listening to you either*.

"Jules, I want you to go on thirty dates in thirty days," Malcolm continued, and this time he was talking fast. "It will be great for our advertising campaign."

"Thirty dates in thirty days?" My voice rose, and I jumped up. "Are you joking?"

"Well, no…" Malcolm cleared his throat. "We'll give you a week to get ready and you will have a discretionary budget of five hundred dollars to buy some new clothes and get to the hairdressers and stuff."

"What's wrong with my clothes and hair?" I glared down at him, huffing and puffing. I didn't even bother asking him what "and stuff" meant. I didn't want to know.

"Well, he knows how many dates they've gotten you thus far." Nolan slid into the conversation and I just ignored him.

"Ugh. I just can't right now." I shook my head and walked toward the door. "I'm going home for the rest of the day. All of a sudden I feel really sick."

"But, Julia, we weren't finished with…" I didn't hear the rest of Malcolm's conversation because I slammed the door behind me as I walked out. When I'd gone to college and studied journalism, I hadn't imagined that this was how I would be spending my days. Not at all.

I HURRIED TO MY DESK AND GRABBED MY PHONE AND handbag and left the office and made my way down to the coffee shop in the lobby of the building. I was all over the place right now. Not only had it been a shock to see Nolan looking at me so smugly, but I was also feeling a little excited. I pulled out the letter that I'd received in the mail that morning and smiled to myself as I reread the note that had been sent to me.

Dear Julia,

How are you today? Well, I hope. I'm sure you're wondering why I'm starting this letter so formally, but I thought that was the best way to start again after so many years. Have still kept my previous letters? I was wondering if you were still single and if you would be interested in meeting me after all these years (though I know you don't know who I am). Maybe we can get to know each other before you decide.

Always Yours,

Fitz

My secret admirer was back. Well, at least I assumed it was the same guy. He did use the same name as he had in the previous letters. Letters that I'd read over and over again. I still had no idea who he was, but I very much wanted to meet him. I couldn't believe that he had started writing me again. It almost made up for the fact that Malcolm wanted to embarrass me in front of the entire town of Canyon Beach and have Nolan Montgomery record it for infamy.

※   2   ※

"**W**here are you?" I almost shouted into the phone as soon as Betsy answered.

"Um, I'm at work," she said and I could hear the sound of a customer asking her something about cupcakes in the background. Betsy was the co-owner of a small cupcake shop with her grandma Elsie and I loved the perks of being her best friend; though my waistband didn't feel quite the same as my lips.

"Your brother sucks," I continued, ignoring the fact that she was at work and most probably had to focus on her customers. I wouldn't normally bother her while she was working, but this was a disaster. Almost on national disaster level.

"Oh no, what has he done now?" Betsy groaned into the phone. "No, Harriet, none of the cupcakes are calorie free, I'm afraid." I heard her talking to one of her customers and I knew that she was busy, but I was too full of fury to hang up and let her get on with her job. Anyway, Harriet sounded like an idiot. Who went to a bakery and expected a calorie free cupcake? I conveniently forgot about the time I went on the

Keto diet and asked Betsy how many of her cupcakes were under twenty grams of carbs (The answer turned out to be none).

"He's only following me now," I said dramatically to get her full attention.

"He's what?" The tone in her voice changed to one of shock. "Not like that creeper in *YOU*?"

"Sorry what?" I was confused for a second and then I remembered the show we'd watched on Lifetime a couple of weeks ago about some creepy stalker guy. It had been really good, but I'd been really tired and fallen asleep during many of the episodes. "No, not that kind of following," I said impatiently. "Even Nolan isn't that crazy. If I found out he was following me, following me, I would kick him in the balls."

"Jules, I'm not trying to be funny here, but what other kind of following is there?" she spoke in a patient tone, even though I was pretty sure I was already getting on her nerves.

"He's following me at work..." I exclaimed waiting for her supportive gasp.

"What? I'm so confused right now," she said in what had fast become an exasperated voice. "No, Harriet, none of the cupcakes are fat-free, I'm afraid."

"Fat-free?" I giggled into the phone. "It's not that Harriet we met that time we went to Weight Watchers is it?"

"Yes," she said in an amused tone. "Jules, as much as I would love to hear how and why my brother sucks, I'm going to have to wait for the information. We're pretty busy in the store right now and it's just me working."

"Do you want me to come by and help?"

"To help or to talk?"

"Both, duh." I giggled, already feeling slightly better. Betsy was my non-sexual other-half. Whenever I was feeling stressed or down, all I needed to do was talk to her to start to get balanced again. And sometimes, she didn't even have to say much. Just knowing she was there for me was enough. I knew I was blessed to have her as a best friend; even though she came with an asshole brother. I guess no one is perfect. "I got another letter by the way."

"A letter?" She sounded confused.

"From Fitz," I said.

"The guy from high school?" This time she really did sound shocked and I grinned. "The one that had the crush on you?"

"Yup."

"No way."

"Yeah, I haven't heard from him since college."

"I wonder if it's that guy Lucas, like we thought back in the day."

"I don't know, but we can discuss later."

"Okay, Jules, come down to the store and don't forget to bring the letter," she said and I hung up with a small laugh. I knew the letter would draw her attention. Betsy was a big romantic, just like me.

"HEY, HEY, I'M HERE," I SANG OUT AS I WALKED INTO Betsy's & Elsie's Yummy Cupcake Store and looked for my best friend's long blond hair behind the counter.

"Hello, Jules," a deep voice called out to me from a back table and I looked over and saw the familiar police uniform of Jefferson Evian. I stifled a groan as I saw Nolan's best friend. What was he doing here?

"Hi, Jeff," I said as I walked toward him slowly with a small smile. "Have you seen Betsy?"

"She just went to find me some chocolate she said she had hidden to make me a special hot chocolate." He grinned and I tried not to roll my eyes. I was going to have to talk to Betsy to see if her high school crush on Jeff had resurrected. I sure hoped not. He was as bad as Nolan.

"Oh okay," I said as I stood there awkwardly, staring down at his dark hair and sparkling blue eyes. "So how are you?" I asked politely, hoping Betsy would hurry up.

"I'm fine, Jules. And you?" He grinned up at me. "Getting ready for your dates?"

"Ugh." I glared at him. "Nolan told you already?"

"Yeah, I had lunch with him, right before he headed to the paper."

"He's got such a big mouth." I just shook my head, my long brown hair flying around my shoulders. "He's going to ruin all of my dates."

"I don't think that's your biggest problem."

"Oh?" I frowned at him. "What's my biggest problem?"

"You seem worried about Nolan following you on all these dates, but what if you don't get any?"

"You're an asshole." I hit him in the shoulder and hurried to the counter. "Betsy, where are you?" I shouted toward the kitchen door.

"Shush, Jules, you're going to scare off all the customers." Jeff stood up and walked to the counter, as well.

"You're the only customer here and I wouldn't mind scaring you off."

"Is that any way to talk to an officer of the law?" he said as he gave me a stern face. "I could arrest you, you know?"

"Arrest her for what?" Betsy chose that moment to come waltzing through the kitchen door, her blond hair hanging straight down her back and her cheeks flush with pink. Her blue eyes looked back and forth at me and Jeff and she gave us an impish grin. "Don't tell me, Jules went and stole a cupcake again?"

"I didn't steal a cupcake," I said at the same time that Jeff pouted and said, "She hit me."

It was then that I froze in shock, not because he was complaining that I'd hit him, but because Betsy gave him a look of sympathy and rubbed his shoulder over the counter. My heart started thudding as I saw Jeff giving her pitiful puppy dog eyes. What the hell was going on here? I'd never seen the two of them acting like that before. And if I had anything to do with it, it wasn't going to be happening for very long. I couldn't stand Jeff and he couldn't stand me. The last thing I needed was for Betsy to start dating him.

"I didn't hit you," I said finally, hoping to break the moment up as soon as possible. I needed to talk to Betsy more than ever now and there was no way that it was going to be in front of Jeff. "You're just as bad as Nolan. Betsy, I really need to talk to you." I gave a pointed look at Jeff and then said. "Alone."

"Oh Jules, what is going on?" Betsy's cheeks looked very rosy and pretty. My eyes narrowed as I noticed that she had makeup on. Betsy never wore makeup. Not even when I dragged her out to go dancing. What was going on here? And what did she mean what was going on? She knew what the hell was going on. Her brother was trying to ruin my life and the great love of my life, Fitz was back (Yes, I didn't exactly know who he was, but if his letters were anything to go by, he was a real sensitive sort of guy).

"Are you leaving now?" I turned to Jeff, even though I saw the little container of Belgian chocolate that Betsy used when she made us hot chocolate. I didn't care that Jeff had been waiting on this special treat. Betsy was my best friend, and this was an emergency.

"I wasn't planning on it." His voice was dry, and I gave him my best, "please leave now" look. Didn't he have work to be getting on with? Cases to be solved or something. "But I'm guessing you want me to go?"

"What gave me away, Sherlock?" I asked and I could see

an aghast look on Betsy's face at my words. "Just joking," I lied, but I didn't want to seem rude and have Betsy all mad at me. Not that I normally cared what Jeff thought about me. He was just as bad as Nolan, but I knew that Betsy cared and I didn't want to make her upset. Especially not when I wanted to moan about Nolan to her. Normally, it wouldn't be a big deal, but I was cognizant of the fact that at the end of the day, he was still her brother.

"Uh-huh." He gave me one of his, "sure, you are," faces, but then I saw him glancing at his watch for a few seconds and he sighed. "You're in luck, Jules. I have to get back to work."

"Back to solving all the crimes of Canyon Beach, then?" I faked an impressed look. "All the serial killers and psychopaths?"

"Jules, you should count yourself lucky that you live in a town with no crime," he said with a shake of his head. "Because if this were a big city, I have a feeling the serial killer would be coming for you first."

"That's a horrible thing to say." I made a face at Betsy then, how could she like this guy? "Really horrible."

"You're such a drama queen, Julia Gilbert." He grinned and then patted the top of my head. "Drama Queen, with a capital *D* and a capital *Q*."

"What's your point, Jeff?" And then because I couldn't stop myself, I said, "Why don't you and Nolan go and take a long walk off of a short cliff."

"When did you graduate from high school again?" He rolled his eyes and then muttered under his breath, "No wonder you need help getting a date."

"I do *not* need help getting any dates, thank you very much."

"What dates?" Betsy gazed at me with a confused expression on her face. "You have a date?"

"No, not exactly," I mumbled under my breath. "I have to go on some dates for my job. Malcolm wants me to write an article about dating. And he's going to have me followed and photographed. By your brother." I sighed loudly. "I can't believe my bad luck. Why me?"

"Oh my." Betsy's eyes widened, and she looked like she wasn't sure whether to laugh or cry. "Go behind the counter and grab a cupcake and then we can discuss more. Let me just say goodbye to Jeff."

"Okay." I smiled at her gratefully. "I knew you would understand. Bye, Jeff." I turned my nose up at him and headed behind the counter and perused the selection of cupcakes. My mouth started watering as I gazed at the different flavors: red velvet, chocolate, chocolate mint, lemon, strawberry, peanut butter cup, I could go on and on. Each and every cupcake looked absolutely delicious. "Oh my God, Betsy, I want all of them." I licked my lips eagerly as I debated between my two favorites, red velvet and chocolate mint. She added half of an Andes mint to the top of the chocolate mint cupcake and that just made it even more yummy.

"Take whatever you want. I'll be right with you." She walked to the exit with Jeff and my eyes narrowed as I watched them whispering about something. What was going on here?

"OH JULES." BETSY TRIED TO CONSOLE ME AFTER I'D TOLD her about my morning. "It will be okay. Maybe it will even be funny."

"Funny?" I paused mid-bite and questioned her. "What do you mean by *funny*?"

"Oh no, I don't mean funny. I mean fun." She giggled. "It might even be fun."

"Nolan is just going to make fun of me." I groaned. "He loves to make fun of me. He's just going to be sitting there with his camera judging me and laughing at me," I wailed as I thought of the smug look on his face just sitting in a corner watching me.

"He won't judge you," she said uncertainly and then made a face. "Okay, he won't judge you too much then. I hope."

"Betsy, this is Nolan we're talking about. Your brother spawn. He has judged us our whole lives."

"I know." She gave me a sympathetic glance. "To be fair though, it's always seemed to me that he treats you like a sister even more than he does me. He always seems to be a lot harsher and meaner to you."

"Right? He's horrible, and he's not even my brother."

"Well, he's close to your brother." She grinned at me. "We're like sisters."

"You will always be my sister, blood or not." I grinned back at her. "Best friends forever."

"Sometimes, I wish that you and Nolan would get married and then we'd be related legally as well." She grinned ruefully.

"Never going to happen," I almost shouted. "He would be so lucky to even have me look at him, let alone anything else."

"I know, I know." She laughed. "You guys are like chalk and cheese." She started laughing then. "I do have to admit I'm surprised Nolan took this job. He has always hated you dating." She rolled her eyes. "It's like he thinks we're still little kids."

"Well, he seems to be all about me dating now." I thought back to his smug face in Malcolm's office. "Ugh, I can't stand him."

"Is that your phone making that noise?" Betsy asked me

and I heard the familiar sound of a grasshopper letting me know that I had some new text messages.

"Oh yeah, I didn't even hear." I pulled my phone out and noticed that Nolan was texting me. My heart skipped a little beat until I saw what his message read.

"Hey, big nose. We should discuss a plan. Free for dinner?"

"No."

"Is it because I called you big nose?"

"You're so rude, asshole."

"I hope you don't talk to your potential dates with that mouth or you're going to be single for a long time."

"Ugh. I cannot stand your brother." I showed Betsy the texts and she laughed. "It's not funny. He's so rude."

"You know how Nolan is."

"How dare he call me big nose." I touched my nose self-consciously. "I do not have a big nose."

"He calls me big ears." She grinned at me. "That's just his way to show you he loves you."

"I'll show him who loves who. Imagine if I called him small dick."

"Jules." She giggled and threw her hands up over her eyes. "He's still my brother, I don't want to even think about his manhood."

"I don't want to think about him period," I whined. "Why is this happening to me?"

"Come over for dinner tomorrow night with my parents and we can discuss this further," she said thoughtfully.

"Will Nolan be there?" I asked, though I already knew the answer. The Montgomerys had a family dinner every week and both Nolan and Betsy were always there if they were in town. I went a couple of times a month and loved to spend time with them all, even when Nolan irritated me. But this was something different. I didn't want to discuss my work problem with her family, when Nolan was half of the problem.

"Yes, and Jeff will be there as well."

"Great, just great," I said sarcastically, my mind too preoccupied with my own issues to ask her what was going on with her and Jeff.

"I know you don't want to talk to them about it, but you know Nolan will be on your case to discuss it and this way you don't have to do it one-on-one. I can run interference for you."

"I guess that's true." I didn't really want to have to talk about it with Nolan at all, but if it had to be done, it would make me feel better to have Betsy there. It would stop me from killing him if he got on my nerves too much.

"So tell me about Fitz," she asked me changing the subject. "Let me see the letter."

"Okay," I said and pulled the letter out of my handbag for her to read. "Do you really think it could be Lucas?"

"I really do. Remember, he was always so shy in school, but I'd always catch him staring at you and I heard he's back in town."

"Oh? Didn't he get married or something?"

"He's divorced now!" she said. "Did I forget to tell you? Grandma Elsie told me, you know she's friends with his grandma."

"Oh wow, no, you didn't tell me." I thought back to the boy we'd known in high school. Lucas had been really tall and skinny, with big blue eyes and dark hair. He'd been a bit of a loner, but he and I had connected over our love of British literature. We were both bookworms and I had thought he was sort of cute in a low-key way. However, he had gone off to Brown University and I'd never seen him again after graduation; though I did wonder if he'd seen me. I had received two letters from "Fitz" when I was in college, but then he had just dropped off of the face of the earth.

"Yeah, supposedly the wife cheated on him with her personal trainer or something and now he's back. He's going to teach English at the high school."

"No way." I was shocked. Maybe it was Lucas after all. "Do you think I should meet him?"

"Yeah, definitely." She grinned. "Also, this is the first time he's left a return address, right?"

"Yeah, but it's just a PO Box." I sighed. If he had left his real address I would have been driving to the location to lay in wait to see who left the house.

"Pity, we totally could have checked it out if it wasn't."

"I was just thinking that." I giggled and we both laughed.

"That's why we're best friends." Betsy handed me another cupcake and I took it happily.

"Yes, but that's also why you can't date 'Wannabe Sherlock.' I gave her a look. "We could never do all the things we'd want with him around."

"Oh, Jules." She just laughed and then gave me a quick hug. "Go home and write your return letter and I'll talk to you soon. I've got to get some work done here."

Dinner at the Montgomery's was always a big and delicious family affair. I'd been coming for years now and always left with a full stomach and leftovers for days. In the past couple of years it had mainly been just me, Jules, her parents, and Grandma Elsie; with Nolan popping in every now and then. This was one of the first nights Jeff had shown up and I wasn't pleased about it at all. I certainly didn't need to see both he and Nolan's smug faces staring at me as Betsy and I discussed my work dilemma.

"I know you're upset about this new series you have to write, Jules, but look on the positive side. You're going to have a lot of exposure. Everyone in town will be reading your column and watching your videos. You'll become famous," Betsy said in a positive tone, trying to make me feel better about my life, but it wasn't really working.

"This is not something I want to become famous for." I knew I sounded like a bratty little kid, but I couldn't stop myself. "And everyone in Canyon Beach talking about my dates over their dinner table is not me becoming famous. That's just everyone knowing my business."

"Think of it as some sort of adventure," Betsy said in her most encouraging voice. "I bet it will turn out to be a lot of fun."

"As much fun as having a tooth pulled out."

"I think going on thirty dates in thirty days will be really exciting." Betsy grinned at me encouragingly, as we sipped on the Earl Grey tea her mom had made us after dinner. "Just think, you might meet Mr. Right."

"Why don't you swap places with me then? You do the articles and I'll make the cupcakes," I said quickly, the idea forming in my brain as I spoke. This could actually be the perfect solution to my problem. I grabbed an oatmeal and chocolate cookie from the plate and took a bite, enjoying the warm sugary goodness in my mouth. Betsy had definitely gotten her baking skills from her mom.

"You can't bake for shit, Jules." Jeff's face looked tight as he spoke. "And you really don't have the right temperament to be selling anything."

"Whatever, I didn't say I'd be selling them." I turned away from him, feeling annoyed. I would much rather not have had this conversation with Jeff and Nolan in my presence. "Why don't you join up to the dating site with me, Betsy? It will make it a much funner experience."

"I think it will be a fun experience with it just being you," Nolan said as he sipped from his beer mug. I was going to make a snide comment about him wasting his mom's freshly brewed tea, but I kept my mouth shut. "I don't know that this town is ready for both of you to go crazy on the dating sites. One psycho at a time is all it needs."

"You're so rude." I resisted the urge to stick my tongue out at Nolan. He was insufferable, irritating, condescending and just an all-around jerk. I had to remind myself I wasn't a teenager anymore. "And really, it takes one to know one. So, if I'm a psycho, you're a frigging serial killer maniac."

"That wasn't nice, Nolan," Betsy said with a half-frown. "Maybe I will sign up as well." She gave me a little wink, and I smiled at her hopefully.

"Really?" Jeff's voice was sharp. "Do you really have time to be dating? Shouldn't you be concentrating on your business? Didn't your grandma Elsie put a lot of money into it?"

"Excuse me?" Betsy looked offended as she turned to Jeff and I hid a smile. If there was one thing you never did with Betsy was to infer that she wasn't a hard worker or to bring up Grandma Elsie. Jeff was about to go down and I couldn't wait to see it. He needed to get off of his high horse. Just because he was a cop didn't mean he was the boss of everyone. He and Nolan both needed to be brought down a peg or two.

"I'm just saying that I don't think there are any men in the city good enough for you to date." Jeff shrugged as he grabbed a cookie. I tried to stop myself from rolling my eyes at his comment. He was really trying to suck up hard, and it was so annoying that Betsy just wasn't seeing it.

"I agree, there is no one in this town good enough for you." I grinned happily as I looked at Jeff, whose face was looking even more sour. "Not a one." I looked at Jeff and winked. "Not even you," I mouthed to him and he just took a gulp of beer. Nolan raised his eyebrows at me and I could see him studying my face carefully. I had no idea what his problem was or why he was giving me that look, but it was getting under my skin the way his eyes seemed to be all-seeing and all-knowing. It reminded me of when we were kids and his uncanny ability to always know when I was lying or upset. I didn't need him trying to analyze me now.

"I think I'll leave the dating to you, for the time being." Betsy gave me a small smile. "I have a lot on my plate right now."

"Well, it's not like I'm really dating. These dates are just part of the job."

"But as a good reporter you really have to get into it." Nolan smirked. "I seem to recall that you have no problem getting into character for a role."

"Whatever." I blushed then as I gave him a sharp look. I knew he was referring to that one night. The incident that was burned into my brain. The incident that I'd never told a soul about. Not even Betsy; especially not her. How could I tell her I'd kissed her brother while pretending he was Romeo? How could I tell her that he was the star of my bedroom fantasies? There was just no way!

"Huh, What are you talking about, Nolan?" Betsy then looked at me. "What's he talking about, Jules?"

"I have no idea." I feigned ignorance and pretended to yawn. "Anyway, it's been a long day. I should be leaving now. Got to get up early and all that jazz." I stretched my arms and stood up. "Tell your parents thanks for dinner and I'll see you all soon."

"Bye, Juliet," Nolan whispered as he looked up at me and my entire body flushed with heat as I remembered the semester I played Juliet in the school play. The same semester I'd asked Nolan to help me overcome my "fears" of the play. The same semester I'd asked him to teach me how to kiss. I looked away from him quickly as I remembered everything I'd asked him to teach me and my face burned red. Oh God, why had I stayed in this small town?

❧ 4 ☙

"Heathcliff." I sighed as I gazed at my black Labrador lying on his back waiting to be tickled. "What am I going to do?" I groaned as he just lay there, his tail wagging, waiting for me to walk over to him. "I'm going to embarrass myself, I just know it." I sat down on the side of my bed and rubbed his belly. He closed his eyes and smiled in satisfaction as he wiggled on the bed. "I cannot believe that Nolan is going to be a witness to all of my dates. This is going to be awful," I continued talking to Heathcliff, but from the look on his face, he had no sympathy for me. "I'm going to have to call, Stella." I reached down to grab my phone from the inside of my handbag. Heathcliff opened his eyes and looked at me in disappointment as I pulled away from him. "Sorry, Heathcliff, I have an emergency right now." I gave him my best smile, but he just ignored me.

"You up?" I text Stella. I looked at the time and groaned. It was only nine o'clock, of course, she was up.

"Yes, what's up?" She texted me back immediately. Stella was always near her phone unless she was at her store. She owned a small bookstore in town and she was the only person I

knew that was even more of a romantic than me. Stella was my slightly younger cousin. Her head was always in the clouds, which made her the wrong person to talk in most situations. In this situation, I needed someone like her to help me feel more positive about the whole situation.

"Work emergency! Call me."

"Give me five minutes. Just need to make sure I'm recording The Bachelor."

"You still watch that show?"

"As if I could ever stop. :)"

I put the phone down on the bed and laughed to myself. Stella was addicted to watching reality TV shows; especially those that focused on dating. Though she rarely ever dated. She was caught up in her books and TV shows, so much so that no man could ever live up to her expectations.

Ring. Ring. I grabbed the phone and immediately started talking. "Oh my God, you will not believe what's happened to me," I screeched into the phone and continued without giving her an opportunity to answer. "Malcolm has assigned me to write a series of articles about dating and Nolan, yes Nolan, is going to be following me on all my dates? What have I done to make God treat me like this? I'm about ready to quit and move. You down to move to Bali with me?"

"Depends on if you're paying," A low deep voice answered me and my breath caught as my heart froze.

"Stella?" I half-whispered, hoping my ears were playing tricks on me.

"Not unless my parents lied to me about my name?" he responded with a chuckle. "Though I think I look more like a Nolan than a Stella, don't you?"

"Nolan Montgomery, what are you doing on the phone!" I shouted. "Don't you know it's rude to, to..." I sputtered and then paused as I didn't know how to end that sentence. "Well, what do you want?" I said finally, indignantly.

"I thought that maybe you and I should talk—"

"I don't have anything to say to you," I interrupted him, my heart racing. I didn't want him to bring up any incidents from the past again.

"I thought it would be helpful. This is just business, Jules. You should stop taking everything so seriously."

"My job is serious and so is my dating life."

"Well, you don't really have much of a dating life, do you, so maybe this will help you."

"You're so rude, you know that right. You don't know what sort of dating life I have."

"Oh?" He sounded surprised. "Are you secretly dating someone I don't know about?"

"Maybe," I lied.

"Is it someone you met online?" he continued. "Have you ever seen him?"

"What?" I asked in a confused tone.

"I'd hate for you to be Catfished. I know how impressionable you are."

"What?" This time my voice was a lot louder. "What are you talking about?"

"That's the only reason I can think of that you would be dating someone and not have told the whole world as yet... you haven't met him yet."

"Nolan Montgomery, if you were not my best friend's brother, you would be fired. So fired."

"Ha ha ha, sorry, I couldn't resist. So tell me, who's this hottie you're seeing?"

"I'm not seeing anyone," I said in a low tone. "Well, not yet. I do have a secret admirer that seems to be really interested."

"Oh?" He sounded bemused.

"Yes, his name is Lucas, and we went to high school together and he's been sending me love letters for years."

"Lucas Sacramento?" He sounded surprised. "Lucas has been sending you love notes?"

"Yes," I said, even though I wasn't one hundred percent sure it was Lucas, but I would find out soon enough. "In fact, I have to write him back a letter tonight."

"Conversing via mail?" Nolan laughed. "Sounds very romantic."

"It is."

"And he signs his letters, Lucas?" Nolan asked lightly.

"As opposed to what?"

"All my love, Lucas, or your darling, Lucas," he drawled.

"He actually signs them Fitz."

"Fitz?"

"I don't know why," I admitted. "Anyway, what do you care?"

"Just curious as to how and why you assumed the letters were from Lucas, but I guess if that's what you're hoping for. I guess that makes you happy."

"Who are *you* seeing?" I said, not appreciating his condescending tone.

"I am concentrating on my career right now. I don't have time for crazy women."

"Oh yeah, your budding career as a filmmaker. I'm surprised you haven't moved to Hollywood yet."

"I have my reasons for staying."

"Oh? You want to terrorize me, huh?"

"Yeah." He chuckled. "I'm staying just for you."

"Whatever." I sighed. "Anyway, I'm waiting on a call from, Stella. What do you want?"

"Want to grab lunch tomorrow? We do need to create a plan."

"I guess so," I said reluctantly. I didn't really want to meet up with him one-on-one. We never really hung out one-on-one. In fact, the last time I had been with him for longer than ten minutes were those times in high school and look how that had turned out.

"Okay, I'll text you tomorrow to figure out a spot."

"Okay."

"Night, Jules."

"Night, Nolan." And as I hung up the phone, I couldn't stop myself from smiling. It wasn't that I wanted to go to lunch with Nolan or see him. I couldn't stand him, but a part of me was excited to spend time with him. I groaned into my pillow as I realized that I still found him to be quite hot. "Get over it, Jules," I muttered into my pillow. "You better not get another crush on him." My face flushed as I thought about how embarrassed I'd felt after our "kiss," well to be fair, I was more embarrassed about what I'd said after the kiss.

Ring ring. I grabbed the phone and spoke hesitantly into the receiver.

"Stella?"

"Yeah. Why do you sound like you just saw a ghost?"

"Ugh, Nolan just called me and I thought it was you."

"Didn't you look at the screen?"

"Nope."

"Why not? It's right there in front of your face."

"Not helping, Stella."

"Ha ha, sorry. So what did Nolan want? I didn't know you guys talked on the phone," she said excitedly. She'd known I'd had a huge crush on Nolan in high school. She just didn't know everything that had gone down between us.

"He just wants to meet up tomorrow to talk about this article series we're working on together."

"Oh, you're working on a series together?"

"Well, kinda." I quickly explained to her what Malcolm had proposed and how opposed to it all I was. "So what do you think I should do?"

"What do you mean what should you do?" She sounded

confused. "It's your job, you have to do it." She paused then. "However, I do have a really great idea."

"Oh yeah? What's the great idea?"

"Let's have a makeover party?" The words tripped out of her mouth. "A makeover party to create your profile." Her voice started rising as she became more and more excited. "It will be great. You, me, Betsy, maybe Abby?"

"That could be fun." I pondered the idea. "What do you mean by makeover though? I don't want to end up with pink hair or something."

"Nothing like that." She giggled. "Just maybe a new haircut and some new clothes, not to be rude, but you always dress so tomboyish, maybe a couple of skirts and dresses, and maybe some makeup."

"So a whole new me, then?"

"Something like that. What do you say? It'll be fun."

"I guess so. And you guys will help me create my profile?"

"Did you even have to ask? This will be so much fun. I bet you meet the love of your life. Could you imagine? It will be the first wedding in our family in years."

"Stella Gilbert, you're getting so carried away." I laughed. "I haven't even gone on a date yet, I'm so far from getting married, it's not even funny."

"Well, with our help, you'll soon be on the way." She sounded happy, and I frowned.

"What help are you thinking about, Stella?" I asked slowly. She sounded way too happy for someone who had just suggested giving me a makeover.

"Well, I was thinking about writing a book, a dater's handbook, so to speak and maybe we could test it on you."

"A dater's handbook?"

"Yeah, for example, I was thinking, what if you dressed up in a sexy negligee and …"

"Stop right now." I laughed into the phone. "I'm not going on any date dressed in any sexy negligee, I'm not a stripper."

"I know you're not a stripper, but what if you tried to sex it up a bit. I've got this idea, and I'd love to test it out."

"I think you're going to have to test it out on yourself." I burst out laughing. "There is no way in hell that I'm going to be sexing up my dates with Nolan Montgomery following me around. He'd laugh me out of town."

"Oh, Nolan Montgomery," she said thoughtfully. "I'm honestly surprised that he's interested in doing this with you."

"Why?"

"I just didn't think he'd want to see you going on all these dates?"

"Why would he care? I'm sure he can't wait to laugh at my misfortune."

"Really?" She sounded surprised. "I always thought he had a thing for you?"

"What?"

"I know, I know. It wasn't something that was super blatant, but I thought he was just shy."

"Nolan is anything, but shy."

"Yeah, true." She laughed. "Oh well, forget him. If he's not going to step up, he doesn't deserve you."

"He doesn't even like me," I said, trying to still the sudden burst of hope that filled me. "And I know that for sure."

"Okay, okay. No need to protest so much." She yawned. "I have an early morning tomorrow, but let me text Abby, and you text Betsy and let's see if we can get together tomorrow night."

"Okay," I agreed. "That sounds like a plan."

"It'll be great. You'll see. Don't worry too much, Jules. This is going to be absolutely amazing."

5

D*ear Fitz,*

    I have to say that I'm very surprised to hear from you, but also very happy. I have always wondered who you are and so I would very much like to meet up with you. Hopefully, you will be able to tell me why you chose that name. It is very unusual. I was going to say maybe you got it from the TV show, Scandal, but then I remembered your first letters came before that show was even out. Did you just recently get back to Canyon Beach? I know that's a weird question, but I haven't heard from you in a while and was wondering if, perhaps, you just had some sort of major life change and moved back.

    Hope to hear from you again soon,

    Jules

I finished writing my letter and put it into an envelope quickly. I knew I'd been a bit full on in my letter, but I wanted Lucas to know that I had a good idea that I knew who he was so that we could end up meeting soon. I wasn't quite sure if I'd be interested in him to date seriously, but it was always worth a try, and I needed a good distraction from my work dates and Nolan. I quickly put a stamp on the envelope, placed it in my handbag and jumped up.

"I'm headed to lunch now, Malcolm," I said as I walked past his office and gave him a little wave. "Nolan and I are going to discuss the articles." I kept my tone pleasant so as to not completely lose it with my boss and get fired. The morning had not started off great. Malcolm had told me about his "brilliant idea" to have the public vote on who I should go on dates with and who I should issue a second date. I had told him that my article wasn't a reality TV show and that the integrity of the paper would be called into question and be considered a laughing stock in Canyon Beach if he allowed such a thing to happen. He had not been impressed with my speech and reaction to his idea and I knew that he was not pleased with the way I'd spoken to him. "Would you like me to bring you back anything?" I asked as I stood at his door.

"A tuna melt would be great, thanks, Jules. I'm so glad you're finally embracing this idea." He beamed at me as if the argument this morning had never occurred. "Here's the company credit card, feel free to put your lunch on the paper as it's a work event." He opened his wallet and pulled out a credit card and I felt extremely guilty for having spoken to him in such a surly fashion earlier when he was going to be so nice.

"Oh no, that's okay," I said as I shook my head, but then he stood up and headed over to me, his eyes warm as he gazed at me.

"Here you go, Jules. I know that you're a little uncomfortable with this idea, but I think it will be great and so do your parents."

"My parents?" I groaned. "You told my parents?"

"Well, it was actually your mother that suggested the idea."

"Oh my God, I could scream." I groaned as I stared at him. "Malcolm, this is so not cool." I had tried to forget that Malcolm and his wife were friends with my parents, he played golf with my dad at the local country club, but this was going too far.

"Well, she didn't suggest the idea for the articles per se, that was all me," he said quickly, knowing that he was getting my mom into major trouble with his words. "Anyway," he said quickly. "Here's the card. Tell Nolan I said hello and feel free to stay at lunch as long as you need to."

"Oh I intend to," I said as I grabbed the card. "I'll need a good few hours to chow down on the lobster and steak I intend to order."

"Now, now, Jules." His face looked panicked. "No need to go overboard. You want to keep your figure nice and trim for all the dates."

"I think I'll add oysters and clam chowder to my list as well." My eyes shot darts at him. "Bye." I slipped the card into my pocket and hurried out of the office. Keep my figure nice and trim? What? He was so bloody rude. I wanted to tell him off so badly, but I knew I couldn't push my luck. My mom on the other hand, well, she'd be hearing from me as soon as I got off of work. How dare she try to use my job to hook me up? She was insufferable. It was like it was her life goal to embarrass me and get me married off. Every time, I went over to dinner, the first topic of conversation was my dating life, as if that was all I had going for me.

"Betsy," I almost cried into the phone as she answered. "Did you get my texts last night?"

"About the makeover?" she asked breathlessly.

"Yeah, can you come? Stella and Abby are going to come and I'm going to need you there to make sure they don't get completely carried away."

"Of course, I'll come." She giggled. "It's going to be amazing. It's such a good idea."

"I didn't realize that I looked that bad."

"You don't look bad, you know that," Betsy said. "Hold on, I have a customer."

"Okay," I said as I walked to the Canyon Beach Diner to meet Nolan. "I'm meeting Nolan for lunch so if you want I can call you back afterward?"

"Sounds good," she said. "Two red velvet cupcakes?" she said to someone. "And a large coffee? Coming right up. Okay, I'll speak to you later, Jules."

"Bye," I said and hung up, pushing my phone into my handbag and increasing my pace. I was slightly late for my meeting with Nolan and I didn't want him to have some smart words for me right from the get-go.

"You made it. I thought you got swallowed by an alligator or a shark or something." Nolan stood up as I approached the table. His green eyes sparkled as his eyes took in my frazzled appearance. I knew I looked a bit of a mess. I'd stopped by the post office to drop off my letter and had had to run for the last ten minutes to not be super late and my hair was now frizzy, my face was red and I was huffing and panting.

"Not now, Nolan." I gasped as I grabbed his glass of water and drank it down hastily. "I need more water," I said as I took the seat across from him. I watched as he sat down again.

"Nice to see you as well, Jules," he said as he looked down at his empty glass of water. "It's a good thing I wasn't dying of thirst."

"Gimme a break, Nolan."

"So how are you? Just run a marathon?" He grinned at me and I stared at his perfect white teeth. "Did you place?"

"Place?"

"Like, did you come in first? I assume you did with the way you're panting."

"I'm not even going to dignify your comment with an answer. Obviously, you know I didn't run a marathon. I was running so I wouldn't be late for lunch with you, but obviously, I wasted my time. I should have just kept you waiting ten more minutes."

"Thank you for running to meet me, Jules."

"Uh-huh," I said as I grabbed a menu. "I'm sure you appreciate it."

"Hey, thanks for meeting me. I'm serious." He leaned forward and grabbed my hand for a few seconds. My gaze flew up to his face in surprise. "I know this is hard for you." He looked sincere and my eyes narrowed at his tone. Was he being serious here? "I'm not the bad guy here, Jules." I stared into his eyes, my jaw almost dropping at his words. I could see specks of gold in his irises and my heart started melting. Maybe he wasn't so bad after all. "I mean, it's not like you get many dates."

"Oh my God." I pulled my hands away from Nolan. "You're absolutely infuriating, you know that, right?" I resisted the urge to stick my tongue out at him. "If you weren't my best friend's brother, I'd..."

"You'd what?" He winked at me. "Kiss me?"

"Arrgghhhhh." I folded the menu and put it down on the table. "I'm so over you. I cannot do this."

"What would you rather be doing?"

"Excuse me?" I blinked at him rapidly. "What does that mean?"

"What does what would you rather be doing mean? I always knew you were a bit slow, but..." He burst out laughing as I glared at him. "Sorry, Jules. You're so easy to wind up, I can't help myself."

"Making fun of me should not be your favorite activity." I continued glaring at him.

"Can I help it if you're my favorite?" He leaned forward and for a few seconds we just stared at each other.

"Whatever, let me see what I want to eat," I said flustered as I opened the menu again. "So what did you want to talk about?"

"I just wanted to make sure that you were doing okay," he said as he opened his menu. "We'll be together a lot in the next couple of weeks and I wanted to make sure that you were comfortable with this whole ordeal. If you're really not comfortable, then I can speak to Malcolm and see if we can come up with a new suggestion."

"Really?" I just stared at him, not really knowing if he was being serious or not.

"Really." He nodded. "Look, I know that I love to tease you, but you're Betsy's best friend. I've known you since you were a little kid with pigtails and braces. I want to make sure that you're all right. I know you're a bit of a drama queen, but if this really makes you nervous, then I can see what we can do to get out of it."

"You mean it?"

"Yeah."

"But that means you wouldn't have a job either."

"Hey, it's not Hollywood. I'll live." He grinned. "So what's it to be?"

"Cheeseburger and fries," I said. "Oops, you're not talking about food, are you?"

"No, but that sounds good."

"I guess I can see how it goes," I said with a small smile. "I mean maybe it will even be fun. Also, Betsy, Stella, and Abby are coming over tonight to help me get ready."

"Oh, a girls' night." He smiled thoughtfully. "Going to watch a movie?"

"No, we're going to work on my profile," I said, deciding to omit the part about the makeover. He didn't need to know that part. I didn't want him to know that I felt like I needed a new look to get a better guy. Well, I hadn't thought that until Stella had brought it up, but I'd spent the night dreaming of looking like a supermodel, instead of my regular girl next door look.

"Oh, your profile, huh?" He looked amused. "Know what you're going to say?"

"Not really."

"What sort of guy are you looking for?"

"I don't know." I shrugged. "Malcolm wants me to focus on the do's and don'ts of first dates, so I guess I'll test out different techniques." I sighed. "I'll have to think about what to say and do. I'll make a plan tonight."

"So, what would your ideal guy consist of?" he asked me casually, and I watched as he called over a waiter to take our order. I wasn't sure if he was really interested or if he was making small talk, but all of a sudden I felt slightly uncomfortable.

"I'm not really sure, to be honest." I shrugged and smiled at the waiter as he approached the table.

"Hi, ma'am, sorry for the wait. Would you like a glass of water and another beverage?"

"Yes, please. Can we have two glasses of water, I drank his." I pointed at Nolan as a way of explanation. "I'll also have a Coke, please."

"And you, sir, anything else to drink?" The waiter had a pleasant smile on his face and looked to be about my age; though I didn't know him; which was surprising for a small town like this. He had short blond hair and big blue eyes and there was something about him that seemed familiar. I stared at him for a few seconds trying to figure out where I might have seen him.

"I'll have a Budweiser, please," Nolan stated with a small smile, his eyes on my face as I stared at the waiter.

"And are you both ready to order?"

"Yes, I'll have the cheeseburger, with no pickles, and a side of fries, please."

"How would you like the patty cooked?"

"Medium please."

"And you, sir?"

"I'll have the same as Jules, but no onions, I'll keep the pickles. Patty medium rare please."

"Great, I'll put your orders right in."

"Thanks," I said. "What's your name again? Sorry, I didn't catch it the first time."

"Oh sorry, I might not have told you." The waiter beamed at me and made an apologetic face. He really was quite handsome. "My name is David."

"Nice to meet you, David. You're new here, right?" I continued still trying to figure out why he looked so familiar.

"Yes, I just started working here last week."

"Oh okay, I thought so. I haven't seen you here before, but you look so familiar." I gave him an impish smile, and he just smiled back at me warmly.

"I bet you say that to all the guys." He laughed and then looked down at his order pad. "I should go and put these orders in though."

"Sure, sounds good," I said and watched as he walked away. I turned back to the table after about twenty seconds and I could see that Nolan was staring at me with a frown on his face. "Oh God, what now?" I said as I waited for him to tell me off about something else.

"Practicing your flirting techniques for your dates already?" he said in a surly tone.

"What?" I blinked at him in confusion. "What are you talking about? What flirting techniques?"

"With the waiter?" He continued to stare at me. "You know he could get fired for fraternizing with you."

"Fraternizing with me? What is this the 1980s?" I rolled my eyes. "I asked him his name, dude, if that's flirting then I must flirt with everyone I ever meet."

"Do you?"

"Do I?" I shook my head, feeling really annoyed. "What's your problem, Nolan? Do you just love to rub me the wrong way?"

"I didn't know I was rubbing you in any way." He grinned at me suddenly. "Is that an offer?"

"An offer to rub me?" I blushed as I said the words. "Are you offering to give me a massage?"

"Do you want a massage?" He raised a single eyebrow at me and suddenly his expression looked very devious. "Do you want me to rub you down with hot oil? Is that what you're asking?"

"No, I don't want you to rub me down with hot oil," I said flustered. "That would burn my skin and also wouldn't that get my clothes all oily?"

"You wouldn't be in clothes, dear." He winked at me and I gasped.

"Nolan Montgomery, that is so inappropriate." I knew that my face was bright red, partially from embarrassment, but also partially from being slightly turned on. What would it be like to have Nolan's warm hands all over my body? I blushed just thinking about it.

"I'm just teasing you, Jules. You're going to have to expect to put up with a lot more than that while you're dating, I'm sure."

"Most guys are gentlemen." I glared at him. "They would never say such a thing."

"Keep living under your rock, Jules." He burst out laughing. "I can't wait to take these videos. You're in for a lot of shocks and the readers of the paper are going to be in for a lot of laughs when they read and watch your weekly column."

"Ugh, don't remind me that they'll be watching me as well. It just seems so invasive. I didn't sign up to be a video star."

"Just a radio star, huh?"

"What?"

"Video killed the radio star, video killed the radio star," he sang, and I laughed slightly at his offbeat voice.

"You're such an idiot, you know that right?" I rolled my eyes and then paused as I noticed that David was approaching the table with our drinks. I smiled at him widely as he placed my Coke in front of me and then the beer in front of Nolan.

"So, seeing as I'm new in town, do you have any recommendations of things for me to do or places to go?" he asked me in his friendly tone and I noticed just how handsome and well-built he was.

"What are you into?" I asked him. "There are a lot of water activities because we're next to the beach. So if you like surfing or snorkeling, it's really great. There's also Canyon Lake that's really cool and you can paddle board and kayak there. I know some people like to golf at the country club, there are some escape rooms, some cool bakeries, bookstores, that sort of stuff."

"It might be cool to learn how to surf," he said. "Do you surf a lot?"

"No, she doesn't," Nolan interrupted then with a snort. "Jules rarely goes into the water."

"That's not true." I gave him a harsh look. "But, no I don't really surf. I do boogie-board sometimes though. That's a lot of fun."

"Yeah, it sounds fun." David nodded and then looked at

Nolan and then me again. "So have you guys been dating long?"

"Oh, we're not dating," I said quickly. I noticed that Nolan was looking surly again and stifled a sigh. "We're about to start a new work project together."

"Oh, cool." David looked pleased and was about to say something else, but a couple at the next table was waving him over. "Hey, sorry, I have to get back to work. Your food should be out soon."

"Thanks," I said with a smile and picked up my Coke and took a few sips. "So, was there anything else, in particular, you wanted to talk about?"

"No." Nolan took a sip of his beer. "Not really. When do you think you can have your first date lined up by?"

"I don't know." I shrugged. "I'm not even on any of the apps yet."

"Hmm, okay. Which apps are you going to join?"

"I don't know. I have to decide."

"I guess for the purpose of the articles, you could join as many as possible and then also rank how helpful each app is," he said.

"What do you mean?"

"Well, they always say Tinder is just for hookups right?"

"Yeah, I guess so."

"Well, you can see if that's right."

"I guess. I'm not looking to hook up with anyone though."

"But that doesn't mean that they won't be trying to hook up with you."

"Yeah, I suppose so." Huh, I'd never thought about that. I'd been so nervous about Nolan watching me trying to date, that I hadn't thought about the actual dates I intended to go on. What sort of guys was I going to meet? And what would they be expecting from me? Also, was I supposed to tell them I was a reporter that was writing a series of articles? If I told them from the get-go would they even want to meet me? And if they did meet me, would they even be their real authentic selves? That seemed to be very unlikely. And if they weren't their real selves, then it would completely negate the whole point of the article.

"What are you thinking?" Nolan asked me, his eyes staring into mine curiously.

"That this is going to be a lot more complicated than I thought." I leaned back in the chair and rubbed the corner of my eye.

"Tell me your thoughts."

"Just thinking that it's going to be weird going on dates with guys and not telling them I'm actually a reporter." I nibbled on my lower lip. "And also, once the videos start going up, word is going to get around about what I'm doing."

"Well, it's only thirty dates in thirty days, so you won't be doing it for very long. By the time word gets out, you'll already be done with the dates."

"I don't know about that..." I sighed. "And what about if I want to date for fun, for me, how will that work?"

"What do you mean?" His brows furrowed as he gazed at me.

"I mean, what if I really want to find a boyfriend and want to use online dating? What if I like one of these guys, what happens then?"

"I thought you weren't looking to really date anyone?" His lips thinned. "I thought this was just for the job. Now you're saying that you might actually fall for one of these schmucks?"

"We don't know that they will be schmucks," I said as I took another sip of Coke. "And I mean it would be nice to meet someone." My voice was soft as I didn't really want to talk about my dating life with Nolan. What the hell was going on here?

"I thought you were concentrating on your career right now?"

"I am, but you never know when you might find yourself in a relationship. I mean, between these online dates and Lucas."

"Aww yes," he nodded. "The infamous Lucas."

"He's not infamous." I blushed.

"I didn't even know you were interested in him." He gazed into my eyes with a curious expression.

"Oh I wasn't, but the letters have been so sweet and well, he seems like he would make a great boyfriend. We have a lot in common."

"Oh?"

"He likes books and I like books and well, he's a nice guy."

"He's a nice guy?"

"Unlike you," I said, feeling annoyed at all the questions. "Why are you interrogating me anyway?"

"Was just curious about your letters and love life." He shrugged and started playing with his phone. "It's just something to talk about, Jules."

"Let's not talk about me." I shook my head, grateful to see David approaching with our burgers. "How's your dating life going?" I asked nonchalantly.

"My dating life?" He gave me a long look as David placed our plates on the table. "Thanks, this is good." He nodded at David as he asked if we wanted anything else. I just smiled at David, not wanting to give Nolan an opportunity to make any more snide comments.

"Yeah, are you seeing anyone?" I asked him, wondering if he was still hung up on his last girlfriend, Melissa, a bubbly blonde that I had hated on sight.

"No." He shook his head. "I'm concentrating on my career and other things."

"Oh yeah, Hollywood is calling," I said and then after a few seconds, I said, "What other things?"

"Just life." He sat and picked up his burger and bit into it. "This is delicious," he said, obviously changing the subject. I hid a grin. Obviously, he didn't seem to like to talk about his dating life either. I was going to remember that. If he ever started to try to get too personal, I would ask him what was going on with his love life.

"Yeah, these are yummy," I said as I took a bite of my burger. The juicy goodness of the meat, cheese, lettuce, and special sauce mixing together in my mouth was so delicious that I thought I was going to die of food bliss. I grabbed a fry and stuffed it in my mouth and sat back, suddenly feeling the happiest I had in days.

6

"Hey, hey, we're here." Stella and Abby sailed through my front door hands full of bags, looking almost like twins with their long brunette hair and fashionable clothes. There were two main differences between them, Stella had green eyes and Abby had blue eyes. Also, Stella was only five four and Abby was five eight.

"Are you ready for your makeover?" Stella grinned at me, her perky eager smile making me smile.

"I guess so." I laughed as I waved them into the living room. "Come on through, I have wine and cider and Betsy is bringing cupcakes. And I was going to order some Indian food for dinner."

"Ooh, sounds yummy." Abby rubbed her stomach. "Though, I really shouldn't be eating all that."

"You'll be fine pigging out one night, Abs." Stella put the bags down next to the couch and then leaned down to rub Heathcliff's ears. "Hey Heathcliff, how are you, my darling?" Heathcliff licked her fingers, his brown eyes dancing with happiness at the attention she was giving him. "Come here, my big baby." She started cuddling him and then Abby also

QUEEN OF FIRST DATES

bent down to pet him and his tail started thumping down onto my cream shag West Elm rug with more enthusiasm than I'd seen from him in a long time.

"You guys are spoiling him," I said with a smile as my heart filled with joy. "Okay, what do you want to drink?"

"Do you have any of that Rekorderlig cider?" Stella looked at me hopefully and I nodded.

"I'll have one as well," Abby said with a smile. "I'm so excited for tonight, thanks for including me."

"You're welcome, it will be a lot of fun. I hope." I laughed then as I walked into the kitchen. "Make yourselves at home and I'll grab the drinks." I opened the fridge and grabbed three cans of cider and then headed back to the living room. My phone beeped as I placed the ciders on the coffee table and I grabbed it from my pocket. "That was Betsy, she said she'll be here in a few minutes and she has a surprise."

"Ooh, I wonder what the surprise is?" Stella looked excited. "I wonder if she's going to test some new cupcake recipes on us. That chocolate pistachio cupcake we had last time was divine."

"Hmm, I don't know. Maybe," I said and then I yawned slightly. "Oh man, I'm already feeling slightly tired."

"No *bueno*, Jules." Abby said as she shook her head. "Go and get your laptop and a pen and pad so we can start getting our plan together."

"Ha ha, everyone's not even here and we're already getting to work." I groaned as I headed out of the room to get my laptop.

"Also, change into something casual and comfortable that you don't mind getting wet." Abby continued. "We'll start with the makeover first."

"What?" I pouted. "Do I look that bad?"

"Not at all, but once I'm done with you, you're going to look fabulous."

"Um, what are you going to do?"

"You'll just have to wait and see." She grinned at me and I watched as she pulled a makeup bag out of one of her larger bags and another bag with a bunch of scissors.

"Are you going to cut my hair?" I stilled, horrified at the scissors.

"Just a little trim, to get rid of your dead ends."

"What?" I made a face. "Are you sure this is a good idea? I can go to a hairdresser."

"No, I got this." She looked at Stella and they grinned at each other. "Now shoo, change and bring your laptop out."

"Yes, boss," I mumbled as I headed to my bedroom. "Who knew I had so many bosses in my life? Not me? Why aren't I making more money?" I walked into my bedroom and stared at my welcoming queen-sized bed with the cream cashmere throw beckoning me to it. It would feel like heaven to just get into bed and watch TV right now. I was feeling tired and just wanted to relax. Not to mention that I was extremely nervous at the new look Abby and Stella wanted to give me. Granted, they were both beautiful and glamorous, but I wasn't sure I wanted them changing me too drastically. I heard the doorbell ringing and knew that Betsy must have arrived.

"I'll get it," Stella screamed out from the living room and I proceeded to take my clothes off and change. I grabbed a pair of gym shorts and a tank top and pulled them on quickly. I grabbed a makeup remover wipe from the bathroom and started wiping my face as I walked back to the living room.

"Hey, Betsy, are you ready to paarrtty," I sang as I danced into the living room. I tried to do the robot and then the moonwalk and started giggling as I saw Stella and Abby staring at me with huge grins on their faces.

"Hey, goofy." Betsy laughed as she walked over to me and gave me a hug.

"What's the surprise?" I asked eagerly, already wanting a cupcake.

"I'm here." A deep voice sounded from slightly behind me and I froze. Oh my God, it couldn't be who I thought it was, could it? I turned around slowly, my makeup remover wipe still pressed against my cheek as I looked into Nolan's eyes.

"What are you doing here?" I moaned slightly. "Is this a joke?"

"Well, nice to see you too, Jules."

"We just had lunch." I stuck my tongue out at him. "What's he doing here?" I asked Betsy, trying not to give her an evil stare.

"Well, I thought he could help us."

"How's he going to help?"

"I have a camera." He held up his camera bag, and I groaned.

"There is no way in hell I'm letting you record this to go on the website. No way in hell. *Comprendo?*"

"*Comprendo*," he said with a grin and then he took his camera lens off. "But I'm not here in a work capacity. I'm here to take your photos."

"What photos?"

"The photos of you for your dating profile."

"What?" I shouted. "What photos?" I glared at him and then turned and gave each one of the girls their own individual death stare. "What is he talking about?"

"Jules, you know that you don't have any recent photos," Betsy started, her voice calm as she walked over to me. "You want to have good photos online, don't you?"

"Are you trying to say that all my photos suck?" I pouted then, even though I knew as I said the words that they did suck. I couldn't think of any recent photos that I would want to post on a dating profile. In fact, the best photo I had was from my high school yearbook and that was because it had been one of those glamor shot photos, where I'd been photo-shopped and glossed over to look like some sort of glowing supermodel. Needless to say, I couldn't really use that photo.

"I'm not saying that."

"She's not saying that," Stella chimed in and rubbed my shoulder.

"Well, I'm saying that," Abby said and shrugged as we all looked at her in disbelief. "I'm not trying to be a bitch, but let's be real, Jules, you take goofy photos. You're always sticking your tongue out or doing cross-eyes. That's fun and maybe even include one photo like that, but you need a hot first photo. Something that will make a guy stop and think, whoa, I need to go on a date with her. You're a beautiful girl, men will be clamoring to get with you once they see that."

"I should be mad at you." I laughed. "But right now I just want to take these hot-ass photos that are going to make me the most popular woman in Canyon Beach. I'm not taking any bikini shots though. I'm not hoeing myself out for a date."

"What's wrong with bikini shots?" Abby laughed.

"Nothing if you're a model or a wannabe actress," I said as I looked at her in envy. Abby was beautiful. She could have been a *Sports Illustrated* model with her long dark tresses and big beautiful blue eyes. If she had been anyone else, I would have hated her, but she was also one of the friendliest and nicest people I had ever met. She worked at the Canyon Beach Dog Rescue, but I knew for a fact that she was only paid for half of the hours she worked there. The other hours were considered volunteer hours as they didn't have much of a budget this year and couldn't afford to pay her more.

"You could be a model if you wanted to be," Abby said and I could see that Nolan was holding in a laugh.

"That's not funny, dude." I pointed at him. "Why are you laughing?"

"I'm not laughing," he replied, his face innocent. "Are you going to get changed or are we taking the photos of you in that outfit?"

"Obviously, not in this outfit." I rolled my eyes at him. "Okay, who's doing what?" I glanced at the girls. "Let's get this party started."

"Okay, I'm going to style you," Stella said excitedly. "And Abby's going to do your hair and makeup. Betsy is going to get to work starting your profiles."

"Profiles?"

"Yeah, your dating profiles. She'll sign you up and fill out your basic information and then when we have the photos done, we can upload them and work on your intro together, so we can make sure you sound amazing."

"Oh my God, this is going to take all night."

"A couple of hours' work to find the love of your life is worth it," Abby said as she started pulling out makeup kit after makeup kit from her bag.

"Love of her life?" Nolan raised an eyebrow as he stared at all of us. "Aren't you taking this a little bit seriously?" He then looked me directly in the eyes. "Are you hoping to meet the love of your life on this app?"

"It would be nice to meet someone special," I said, wondering if he'd already forgotten our earlier conversation. "I do want to get married and have kids someday, you know."

"Hmm," he said and before I could ask him what the hmm meant, he had placed his camera on my dark cherry wood coffee table and headed toward the kitchen.

"Hope you don't mind we invited him," Betsy said with a small smile. "I'm sure he'll take beautiful photos."

"I can't say I'm overjoyed." I stared at the camera. "But I guess he's providing a service I'm in need of."

"Yeah, exactly." Betsy looked happy I was coming around. "You'll see, it will be great."

"It will be fantastic," Stella said and gave me a sympathetic smile. She knew just how awkward this made me feel. "Absolutely amazing."

"I don't know about all that."

"Nolan will have you looking like a supermodel," Betsy said, and I just rolled my eyes.

"Don't promise things I can't deliver," Nolan said with a grin and stuck his tongue out at me. "I'm a photographer, not a miracle worker."

"You're so rude." I glared at him, my mind running through all my options of clothes to wear so that I could look the best he'd ever seen me. "No wonder you're single."

"No wonder I'm single, Ms. Queen of first dates?"

"Shh." I stomped to the door. "Come on, girls, help me choose an outfit and do my makeup before I kill Nolan and get sent to jail for life."

"Ha ha, you're so funny." Nolan winked at me and I just tilted my head up and walked to my bedroom, my face burning.

"You look absolutely beautiful." Betsy grinned at me as I stared at my perfectly made up face in the mirror. I looked down at the red dress that Stella had thought would look great on me and then did a little spin. It fit me well and showed off every curve of my body. I grinned at the girls in the room with me; ready to get my photo taken.

"Guys, you have done an amazing job. Let's get these photos done now before I chicken out." I walked to the living room with my heart racing. I knew I looked good, but I wondered if Nolan would even notice.

"It's about time. I almost fell asleep waiting for you to doll yourself up," he said as he got up from my living room sofa. I watched as his eyes widened as he took in my appearance. He stood there for a few seconds just looking me over before his eyes met mine again. I gave him a small smile and waited for him to compliment me in some way.

"You're going to wear that?" He blinked at me, his face serious and stern. My heart dropped at his words.

"What do you mean?" I was confused as I looked down at myself. "Don't you think I look good?" I hated myself for asking him what he thought almost as soon as the words came out of my mouth.

"Good for a Vegas show? Sure," he said as he looked me up and down more deliberately now. "Is this the outfit you want potential dates to see?"

"What are you saying?" Betsy walked up behind me and questioned her brother. "Why are you asking Jules about her outfit? She looks hot."

"But is she going to be looking like that on every date?" he responded. "Or is this some sort of bait and switch?"

"Excuse me?" My jaw dropped. "Bait and switch?"

"Well, you're going to look all hot in the photo and then show up looking like Quasimodo."

"You're so rude." I glared at him, but I couldn't stop myself from singing inside. He thought I looked hot. He didn't want to admit it out loud or praise me, but he'd let it slip.

"Come on, Quasi, let's get you posing."

"You're just jealous that she's hot and you're not," Betsy said and then she turned to me. "Ignore, Nolan. He just wishes he could get a girl half as hot as you."

"Yeah, that's been my greatest wish. To get with Jules." He rolled his eyes.

"That's not even what I said, asswipe." She hit him in the shoulder. "How are you so old and so immature?"

"How are you so old and so whiny?" he snapped back at her and I couldn't stop myself from laughing.

"You do realize that we're in some sort of time warp right now?" I rolled my eyes at both of them. "You're both acting like little kids again."

"One of us still is a little kid," Betsy said.

"Stop talking about yourself," Nolan said with a huge grin and we all started laughing.

"Sorry to love you and leave you," Stella said as she came up behind us with her bags. "But Abby and I are going to head out now, is that cool?"

"Sure! Thanks so much for coming!" I gave them both a quick hug. "You've made me look amazing. I'm going to have so many first dates now."

"Girl, you're going to be the dating queen of the world."

"I don't know about that."

"Well, at least the dating queen of Canyon Beach."

"Yeah, I'll be the dating queen of Canyon Beach." I smiled at the two girls that were beaming in front of me. "Thanks for the makeover. I really appreciate it."

"And now you know how to do makeup for the dates." Abby grinned. "And we left you a bunch of clothes to wear so you look fabulous." She paused for a second. "Not that you didn't already look fabulous."

"What outfits?" Nolan interrupted our conversation with a frown. "Not more dresses like that." He nodded toward me and I could see his eyes darting to my partially exposed breasts.

"What's wrong with this dress?" I asked him, my hands on my hips.

"Nothing," he said slowly, disdain dripping from his tongue. "If that's the look you're going for."

"That's the look she's going for," Stella said and kissed me on the cheek. "Call me in a couple of days and let me know how it's going."

"And email us the photos!" Abby said eagerly. "I'm so excited to see what Nolan comes up with."

"I'm sure he'll make her look even more fabulous," Betsy said as much for our benefit as for Nolans.

"Uh-huh. I don't have all night." Nolan growled and turned back around. "Let's get started." He headed over to his camera, that I noticed he'd set up on a tripod. He turned to look at me and he snarled, "Ready, queenie."

"You don't have to be so rude," I said and looked down at the ground. What was his problem?

"Yeah, Nolan. What's your deal?" Betsy spoke up. "Not funny anymore." She gave me a look and mouthed. "Men." I knew she thought he was just being grumpy, but I felt like there was something else going on here. Something I didn't understand. Did he think that I had gotten dressed up just for him?

"I have no deal." His voice sounded sarcastic. "Let's just get these photos over with. I do have a life and other things to do this evening."

"Like what? Videogames and *Jessica Jones*?" Betsy rolled her eyes as she drawled sarcastically. "I know Netflix can't wait to see you again."

"Maybe I have a date." His words were sharp, and I felt my heart racing as we gazed at each other for a few seconds. He had a date? With who? Not that I was going to ask. I knew that would be all he needed to keep teasing me.

"Then let's get going," I said and licked my lips. "I've got some hot men to meet and date," I said and slowly played with my hair. I watched Nolan as he stared at me for a few seconds, his eyes narrowing at my words. I was sure that he had something else to say, but for some reason, he didn't say anything else. I was a bit disappointed but ready to get the night over and done with.

"I'm going to just take a call," Betsy said, looking slightly suspicious as she held up her phone. "Grandma Elsie wants to talk to me about something."

"Everything okay?" I asked concerned.

"Yeah." She nodded with a smile. "I told her I'd call her tonight, so I better do it now. Be kind to each other, guys."

"Nolan doesn't know how to be kind," I said and she just shook her head.

"I don't know how to be nice?" he said as Betsy left the room. "Really?"

"Really."

"I wasn't nice to you in high school when I gave you your first kiss?" He raised an eyebrow at me and I blushed. "And what about when you were a senior in high school and wanted me to be your first lover as well?"

"Nolan," I screeched. I couldn't believe he was bringing this up now. We had never spoken about that night ever and I certainly didn't want to start now.

"What?" He stepped toward me. "Wasn't I a nice guy then?" His eyes narrowed and he looked down at my lips. "I can still remember the way you pressed your body against mine that night."

"Nolan," I whispered, swallowing hard as I also remembered that night. I still couldn't believe how courageous I had been back in the day. It still seemed like I was in high school when I was around him. I thought back to that night, I'd been sleeping over at Betsy's the weekend after prom and Nolan had been home for the weekend, studying for his finals.

"Hey there, nerd." Nolan grinned at me and my heart skipped a beat. I hadn't seen him at all this year, yet his handsome face still made my heart jump. "How was prom?"

"Good, thanks." I smiled at him as I thought back to our kiss from three years ago.

"Who did you go with?"

"Betsy and a group of friends."

"No boyfriend?" He looked surprised as I shook my head. "Are the guys at Canyon Beach High stupid?" he asked and I could feel my face flushing.

"I guess so." I grinned and he laughed.

"You grew up all right. You know that, right?" His expression was serious for a few seconds as he studied my face. "You're still a kid, but you're not half bad."

"I'm not a kid." His words burned. I remembered him calling me a kid after our kiss and I hated that word.

"Kissing lots of boys now?" He eyes gazed into mine with a curious expression and a touch of something else I couldn't quite read.

"Yes," I lied. I'd only kissed two other boys and none of them had affected me quite as much as Nolan had. "Lots and lots."

"Good," he said with a huge grin, though his smile didn't reach his eyes. "I taught you well."

"Yes," I said as I stared at his lips. "You did." I then did something that shocked both me and him. I leaned forward and kissed him on the lips hard for a few seconds until he was kissing me back. I felt his arm go around my waist and pull me into him. I gasped as I felt his tongue sliding into my mouth smoothly and I felt his fingers inching their way up from my waist. I ran my hands through his hair and pressed myself into him, my body melting into his. I'm not sure what would have happened next because the front door slamming made us jump apart.

"You really have grown up," he said, as he pressed his fingers against his lips. "Who would have thought little Julia Gilbert would be going around kissing men."

"I'm not going around kissing men, I'm kissing you."

"I'm no good for you, Julia. I have needs that include more than a few kisses." He winked at me. "I got to go out. I'll see you later."

"Bye," I said, and I felt a wave of sadness crossing over me as he left. I wanted more from Nolan, but he still thought of me as a little kid. And what needs did he have that I couldn't fulfill? My entire body warmed as I realized what he'd meant. I grinned to myself as I realized that I could fulfill that need. I hadn't had sex before, but not because I was waiting for marriage. If I was honest with myself, no guy had ever lived up to Nolan. It would be perfect if he was my first lover as well as my first kiss.

I could barely stop myself from blurting out my plan to Betsy as I waited to hear Nolan come home. There was no way I could tell her what I was going to do or how special that night was going to be. She just wouldn't understand and I knew that she'd most probably be able to talk me out of it.

My heart was beating so fast that I thought it would pop out of my stomach and run away when I heard Nolan's footsteps walking down the corridor toward his room at around eleven p.m. Betsy was already snoring away as I'd told her I'd been really tired and just wanted to sleep after we'd watched some Friends episodes on her laptop. I got out of the bed slowly and quickly put on some makeup as best as I could in the dark. I pulled off my pajamas and pulled on a white T-shirt that only made it to the top of my thighs. I patted down my hair and headed for the door.

"Screw it," I mumbled to myself as I quickly pulled off my T-shirt so that I could remove my bra and flung it to the ground. I then pulled my T-shirt back on and slipped out of Betsy's room. I hurried down the hall to Nolan's room and took a few big gulps before I opened the door. I couldn't believe that I was doing this. The lights in his room were off as I opened the door and I felt a sense of disappointment as I wondered if he was asleep already. Had I waited too long?

"Jules?" His voice sounded surprised and I could make out his silhouette in the darkness as he sat up. "You okay?"

"Yes, was uh, was just hoping to talk?" I said as I stood in the doorway.

"Sure, come in," he said and I closed the door behind me and crept

to his bed. He flipped on the lamp on his nightstand and I stared at his beautiful naked chest as his green eyes surveyed me. "What's going on?" His expression looked a little dazed and his hair was an adorable mess around his face.

"I just wanted to talk." I sat on the bed next to him and smiled shyly. I couldn't believe that I was in Nolan's bedroom and on his bed.

"Oh?" His eyes looked down at my long bare legs and ran up to my black thong that was visible now that my T-shirt had ridden up slightly.

"Yes," I said and then I reached my hand over to his chest and ran it down to feel his washboard abs. Warmth spread through me as I touched his body.

"Jules." He groaned, and he reached for me and pressed his lips against mine. I melted against him and kissed him back passionately, my hands running through his hair as his tongue invaded my mouth. I ran my hands down his back and I felt his fingers touching my thighs gently, tracing invisible lines up and down. I felt myself shivering at his touch and I stared into his eyes as he kissed down my neck and toward my collarbone. His eyes watched me as his hand moved up the inside of my T-shirt and cupped my breast gently, his fingers teasing my nipple so delicately that I gasped. I licked my lips and fell back as he positioned himself over me and I felt his palm between my legs on my pussy. I squealed as he kissed me again before slipping two fingers inside of my panties and feeling my wetness.

"You wanted to talk, huh?" He grinned against my lips and I grinned back, my hand reaching down to touch all of him. My eyes widened as I felt how hard his cock was.

"I want you to be my first," I said as I kissed him and squeezed my legs tight around his hands. "I want you to make love to me."

"What?" Nolan groaned as he shook his head and sat back on the bed. "Jules." He muttered something unintelligible under his breath, as he pulled away from me completely. "Jules, what are you doing to me?"

"Nothing, yet." I smiled at him innocently and he stroked the hair away from the side of my face.

"I can't do this." He shook his head as his eyes swept over my face and body. "I'm sorry, you should go back to Betsy's room."

"But..." I almost whined. "Please?"

"Jules, you're still in high school." He shook his head. "And you're Betsy's best friend. No."

"I'm going to college in a couple of months."

"Sorry," he said, and he gave me one last long lingering kiss before he jumped up off of the bed. He grabbed my hands and pulled me up. "Now, go back to your own bed, put on a bra and go to sleep." He dismissed me and I walked back to Betsy's room with tears in my eyes. I'd never been so humiliated in my life.

"Just think, I could have taken you that night and given you all sorts of pleasure."

"Nolan!"

"Do you still sleep with no bra on?" He winked at me and I blushed.

"Just take the photos. I'm not answering these stupid questions." I could feel my face burning bright red. I wanted to ask him how many women he knew that slept with a bra on, but I didn't really want to know the answer.

"Stupid questions?"

"That was in the past. I was in high school then."

"But that wasn't the last time though?" he said with a small smile. "I still remember that time you were in college..." His voice trailed off and we just stared at each other for what felt like an eternity. There was no way in hell, either one of us wanted to talk about that night. I was positive about that.

"I'm back," Betsy said, walking into the room at exactly the right time. "How's it going?"

"Great, just great," Nolan said through gritted teeth. "Jules is a natural." And for the next two hours, everything was extremely professional.

"I'll have the photos to you in two days," Nolan said as he packed up his camera and lenses and tripod. "And then you can set your man-trap up."

"Just ignore him," Betsy said as she grabbed me and squealed. "I saw some of the photos on his camera screen and you looked beautiful. I know this dating stuff is for work, but I feel like you could also meet the guy of your dreams. The man that can give you the orgasm of all orgasms."

"Betsy." I squealed embarrassed that she'd said that in front of Nolan. I looked at him for a few seconds and his expression was furious.

"We all can't be Mr. Darcy's, you know." He gave me a poignant look and then he marched out of the living room and through the front door without another word.

7

"How's it going, Jules?" Malcolm gave me a huge smile as he cornered me in the small kitchen.

"Good." I nodded at my cup filled with recently brewed coffee. "Better now."

"Any dates lined up as yet?"

"I'm working on it." I gave him a small smile. "In fact, I just got an email from Nolan with the photos for my profile, so I'll be up and running soon."

"Have the profile up and running by the end of the day," he said, his expression kind, but his voice insistent. "I want these articles online as soon as possible."

"Yes, sir," I said, gripping my coffee cup tightly. I still hadn't gotten used to the idea that I was going to be dating and writing about it. This really wasn't the career I'd seen for myself when I first started working at the paper. The breaking headline stories I'd envisioned were nowhere to be seen. No Pulitzer prize was going to be making its way to my shelf anytime soon. And I couldn't believe that I had to create the profile myself. Betsy had gotten a call and had to leave earlier than planned the night before so we hadn't gotten around to setting up my profiles as yet.

"Now, Jules, I know you weren't happy with this assignment, but I can guarantee that by the time you're done, you'll be thanking me."

"You can guarantee that, can you?" I tried to raise one eyebrow at him, but I knew I wasn't successful as I felt my eyebrows raising up on my face.

"Is something wrong?" He looked at me with a concerned face as I kept wiggling my eyebrows.

"No, no, I'm fine." I sighed and put my eyebrows to rest. "I should go now though and drink my coffee and get my profile set up and all that good stuff," I said and hurried through the door and to my desk. I moved quickly and sat down, grateful to be away from him. I placed my coffee cup on the table and eagerly opened my email account. I wanted to see the photos Nolan had taken of me. I clicked open and waited for the attachments to load impatiently. I was so annoyed at how slowly they were loading. "Stupid Internet," I muttered under my voice, but my breath caught as the first photo loaded.

My eyes almost popped out of my head as I saw the first photo. There was no way that was me. The girl in the photo looked beautiful and radiant. I clicked on the image to see it better and moved my face closer to the screen. "Wow," I said as I stared at the best reflection of myself that I'd ever seen. My skin glowed, my eyes looked bright, the smile on my face looked genuine and the angle of the camera gave me an hour-glass figure that I'd never seen before. I grabbed my cell phone and called Betsy.

"Hey, doll," she answered the phone in one ring. "How's it going?"

"Your brother..." I said breathlessly, unable to say anything else.

"Oh no, what's he done now?" She sounded annoyed. "I swear to God, I'm going to strangle him."

"Nothing, nothing bad. He's just an amazing photographer."

"Oh, you got the photos?" She sounded pleased. "And you like them?"

"They're great," I said happily. "Do not tell him I said that though."

"Don't worry, I'm not about to give him a big head."

"Good." I laughed. "I just wanted to let you know they arrived. I should actually create this profile now though. Malcolm is going to kill me if it's not done by the end of the day."

"Send it to me as soon as it's live. I can't wait to see it."

"Okay." I giggled and then groaned. "Ugh, this is going to suck."

"Think of all the dates."

"I hate dating."

"This will be different. You'll see."

"Ugh, I hope so." I opened a new tab and put in the name of the dating website. "Okay. I gotta go. Talk later."

"Sounds good," she said as I hung up. I looked at the OkCupid website and groaned at all the questions I needed to answer. "This is too much." I whined and went to the app store on my phone and searched for dating apps. The first two that popped up were Tinder and Bumble, and underneath them were Hinge, Coffee Meets Bagel, and Plenty of Fish. I felt tired just looking at all the apps and so I decided to just focus on two, Tinder and Bumble. They seemed the easiest to set up and least complicated to get going. Even though I knew Tinder was the "hookup app," I decided to try it because I knew it was a fast way to meet men. And well, I only needed to go on one date. I could shut them down easily if I had to. And Nolan would be there so it wasn't like they could do anything too crazy.

NAME: JULIA GILBERT

Age: 26

Looking for: Single male aged between 26-33. Preferably 5'8" and taller.

Blurb: Single, fun-loving gal seeking funny, adventurous male for hiking, kayaking, coffee, ice-cream, and romance.

I LOOKED AT MY BLURB, MY EYES SCANNING THE WORDS quickly. "No, no, no, this sucks." I groaned under my breath. No men were going to read this profile and think "ooh, she's the one." I sighed and called Stella's number quickly. I needed help setting up this profile.

"Hey, honey, how's it going?" Stella sounded breathless as she answered the phone and I frowned.

"What are you doing?" I asked suspiciously, my mind in the gutter.

"I'm on a ladder." She giggled slightly. "Stacking a new shipment of books."

"Oh, okay," I said with a little laugh.

"What's so funny?" she asked, her voice tinged with curiosity.

"I thought you were having sex," I admitted and grinned as she burst out laughing.

"You thought I was having sex and still answering the phone?" Stella asked, her voice amused. "I don't know what sort of sex you're used to but I don't have time to answer the phone when I'm in the throes of passion."

"Stella." I rolled my eyes as I looked around the office to

make sure no one was listening to my conversation. "I've had plenty of good sex."

"Oh, I don't think so. No one calls great orgasm inducing sex, *good*," Stella said, and I laughed.

"Well, that's why I need to meet a good man."

"I bet Nolan could give you great orgasms."

"Stella!"

"Sorry." She giggled. "I couldn't resist. He's such a good-looking guy, even though he's such a douche."

"Isn't he just the biggest douchebag?" My voice rose as I thought about Nolan. "He was so rude the other night."

"He was just jealous."

"Jealous of what?" I asked, my heart racing.

"That you're about to meet an awesome guy and leave him in the lurch," Stella said. "Some guys never realize what they've got until it's gone."

"Well, he doesn't have me," I said with a frown. "You know I don't have a crush on him anymore, right?"

"Uh-huh," Stella said, and I was about to pursue the matter of convincing her that I didn't have a crush on Nolan anymore but I stopped myself. What was that saying? When one protests too much, it meant they were really still into that person or something like that. I wasn't going to give Nolan the satisfaction of even uttering his name anymore. He didn't even deserve one more second of thought in my brain. "So what was this call about? I need to start reorganizing the biography and memoir section."

"Sounds exciting," I said and was only partly kidding. I was a little envious of the fact that Stella had her own bookstore. It was something I could see myself doing if I wasn't a reporter. I absolutely loved books more than anything.

"It's so exciting. So what's up?"

"I need help with my blurb for my dating profile. It sounds tired and boring."

"Read it to me," she said and I read it to her quickly.

"Yeah, no," she said as soon as I stopped talking. "You sound fake, like someone with no actual personality of her own. Why don't you craft something truly heartfelt and honest?"

"Really, but wouldn't that make me sound boring?" I asked, thinking out loud. "I love to read under the night sky and sing in the shower along with my dog."

"That's not boring, and that's who you are. If a guy doesn't like that, why bother going on a date with him?"

"Well, this is for my work, not an actual date."

"I think the two are mutually exclusive," Stella said thoughtfully. "I think it's high time you met a good guy and well, your job is even willing to pay for you to meet him."

"You really think I'm going to meet a guy to truly date during this process?"

"I really do," Stella said, her voice sounding more excited now. "I actually have a really good feeling about this."

"Uh-huh."

"Why don't you rewrite the profile, then email it to me and I'll respond with some feedback after I finish stacking these books."

"Okay," I said with a little sigh. "I'll be my full-on honest and boring self."

"You're not boring."

"I am, but thanks for saying I'm not."

"Love you, cuz."

"Love you more," I said with a grin and hung up. I stared at my phone screen and then brought up Word on my computer. I was about to start typing when I realized that what I really needed to do was to use a pen and paper. I always felt more inspired when I handwrote and then typed up my notes into the computer. I grabbed a pen and my yellow legal pad and started writing furiously. About ten minutes later I reread what I'd written and smiled. "This is much better," I said under my breath as I reread the paragraph again.

Some people say the pen is mightier than the sword and I agree. I love the written word. As an avid writer and reader, I'm looking for someone that can appreciate the hidden beauty of the everyday moments that people take for granted.

I like to dance along the sand as the water splashes on my toes. I like to lie in the grass and stare up at the night sky looking for constellations I can't name. I like to sing in the shower to songs playing on my iPhone as my dog sits in the corner, howling along with me. I like to eat pizza, and fries, and then stuff my face with ice cream on a Friday night. I like to go to the drive-in and watch movies in the car. I like to huff and puff as I hike as I'm not as fit as I'd like to be, but I love nature. If you like any of these things, please feel free to say hello.

I smiled as I started typing the words into my dating app. I knew that my paragraph was a bit long and flowery, but any guy that didn't like that wasn't the guy for me anyway. I groaned as I got a message on the app that my blurb was too many characters. I couldn't fit it in. I sighed and then sat back for a few seconds. I hadn't expected this to be so hard. I erased what I'd written and started typing quickly. *Books, stars, sandy beaches, milkshakes, movies, sunrises, sunsets, beating hearts, smiling faces.* I read the very brief sentence and then quickly added, *warm kisses.* I needed it to be a little flirty and cute after all. I needed to match with enough men that I could have frequent dates. I knew that wasn't going to be as easy as Malcolm thought it was going to be. At least not if I had some standards. I didn't want to be one of those people that swiped right on everyone. I quickly posted my blurb to Tinder and Bumble and set up the accounts. I sat back feeling satisfied that I had now launched myself into the world, but then I remembered that I actually had to start swiping on the photos of the guys. I was about to start swiping when my phone started ringing. I looked at the screen and was surprised to see Nolan's name flashing on the screen.

"Hello," I said answering the phone.

"Did you get the photos?" His voice was dry and I could almost see the pompous look on his face.

"I'm doing well, how are you doing?" I said sarcastically.

"Did you get them?"

"Yes..." I said and then reluctantly added. "Thank you. They looked good."

"I worked some magic, huh?" he said with a laugh and I made a face into the phone.

"Whatever, dude." I shook my head at his words. "I guess it would be magic rather than skill that would ensure you took a good photo."

"So when's your first date?" He laughed. "I need to know what evenings I need to block off."

"I don't have any dates yet. You just sent me the photos an hour ago. It doesn't happen that quickly."

"It doesn't? I thought that women got bombarded on these sites."

"I haven't even started swiping yet."

"Oh, okay..." His voice trailed off, and I wondered what he was thinking.

"I'm not going to see you on these sites, am I?" The thought suddenly popped into my head and I was curious as to what Nolan's profile would look like. What would he say about himself? What photos would he use?

"Me?" He scoffed. "Nope, not at all. I don't use dating apps. I meet girls the old-fashioned way."

"Okay, that's why you have so many hot dates."

"Keeping track?"

"Whatever." I rolled my eyes, my cheeks flushing.

"So how's the acting going?"

"What acting?"

"You're not auditioning for anymore roles? I thought you made a wonderful Juliet."

"That was in high school, Nolan." I refused to let him embarrass me. "I've moved on since then."

"You seemed to really put your all into it back then."

"Okay..." My voice trailed off. I wasn't going to rise to the bait.

"So did you hear back from Lucas?" he asked innocently.

"Nope," I said with a small sigh. Maybe my letter was too forward.

"Yeah, maybe asking him if he'd just moved back into town was asking a lot. If he's never told you who he was before, he might want to go a bit slow."

"Yeah, perhaps," I said, not sure what to think.

"By the way, if you're ever in need of any help practicing for your dates... kissing, flirting, making love, that sort of thing, just let me know."

"Goodbye, Nolan," I said coldly and hung up to the sound of him laughing.

"So, ARE YOU READY FOR ALL THE HOT ELIGIBLE MEN OF Canyon Beach to come knocking on your door?" Betsy asked me as I placed a bowl full of spaghetti Bolognese in front of her. It was one of my signature dishes because it was easy and fast to make.

"Yeah, I'm so ready." I made a face at her as I turned around to grab the bowl of salad and homemade garlic bread from the counter to bring back to the table. "I'm sure they are all anxious to knock on my door."

"Come and knock on our door..." Betsy started singing a vaguely familiar tune.

"What's that song again?" I asked her before sitting down

and taking a sip of the red wine that Betsy had brought and poured into two wineglasses.

"It's from *Three's Company*." She gave me an indulgent smile. "An old TV show."

"Oh yeah, yeah, I know it," I said because the name sounded familiar, even if I couldn't actually recall any of the actors that starred in it.

"So, tonight we're going to start swiping?" She grinned. "I'm so excited."

"Ugh, I'm so not excited," I said and then gave her a poignant look. "You also better not swipe on any duds for me. I'm not going to be happy going on crappy dates with crappy guys."

"Jules, half the guys are crappy." She just grinned. "So you can't avoid that. However, I can guarantee you that I'm only going to swipe on men that I think will be interesting in some way or if they're superhot."

"I don't care about superhot."

"But you do need interesting..." she said, and I nodded.

"Yes, I need interesting. These articles have to be really good." I nibbled on my lower lip. "I heard that there's a board meeting for the paper tomorrow. I think Malcolm is really nervous. He's supposedly been going through the advertising numbers and we're down thirty percent from last year." I stifled a sigh. "I've a bad feeling about the longevity of the newspaper."

"You guys have a digital site now, right? So that has to be helping?"

"Yeah, a little bit. Though all of us reporters have really been only focusing on the print side." I felt slightly guilty. "But I think Malcolm wants this series to be on the website."

"Are you okay with that?" Betsy asked softly as she knew that I had always felt like being a print journalist meant so much more than just writing for a dot com.

"You know what?" I said with a small smile. "I guess I am. I mean I don't really want to write this article, or series of articles. I don't want to go on these dates, but I guess it is a way to connect with readers in some way." I made a face. "Ugh, I mean I don't know that this was what I ever wanted to write, but if it's going to help the paper, I guess I'll do what I have to do."

"You're a good person, you know that?" Betsy gave me a wide smile. "And this is absolutely delicious," she said as she mouthed down a forkful of spaghetti. "How is it so yummy?"

"How are you such a good friend?" I laughed. She always complimented my food, even though she was definitely the top chef between us.

"Just remember that when I'm swiping for you." She grabbed a slice of the garlic bread. "Do not question my decisions."

"Betsy, you're making me nervous." My eyes narrowed at her. "Maybe I'm crazy for letting you swipe on one of the apps for me."

"You can't take it back now." She laughed. "No way, Jose. It wouldn't be fair."

"Um, they're my dates."

"And they're my ears that will be listening to all date stories to come." She grinned. "Plus, I'm excited to see if I recognize anyone."

"We'll recognize most people," I said with a groan. The problem with living in a small town your whole life is that everyone knows everyone.

"True, but there are a lot of new people in town nowadays and maybe you'll get responses from guys from out of the area."

"Yeah, and I can count them all on one hand."

"No, you can't." Betsy shook her head. "We don't really go out and mingle but Jeff was telling me that the mayor was a little concerned at the high number of people that have moved to Canyon Beach in the last two years."

"Why?"

"He's scared crime will go up or something." She shrugged. "But I haven't noticed any new crimes or anything."

"Yeah me either." I was silent for a few seconds as I munched on some garlic bread. "So what's going on with you and Jeff then?"

"What do you mean?" Betsy's eyes widened innocently, but I could see a soft flush in her cheeks.

"Do you like him?"

"No," she answered quickly as she looked away. "He's just Nolan's best friend so I see him every now and then and at the store for coffees and stuff."

"Okay," I dragged the word out with a smile. "And stuff, huh?"

"Jules, what are you implying?"

"Me?" I pointed my fingers at myself. "Me? Implying anything?" I grinned at her. "Would I do such a thing? If you, my very best friend in the world, says that there's nothing going on with Jefferson Evian, then of course, I believe you."

"Jules." She groaned. "You suck."

"Why do I suck?"

"Yes, there's been a little flirtation between us," she said as she moaned. "But I don't really know if he's interested, and if he is, I don't know if it would be a good idea for us to date."

"Why?" I blinked, forgetting how much I couldn't stand him for a second.

"Because he's Nolan's best friend," she said. "And he's always been a player, and he's always said he never wants to get married."

"He has?"

"When he was in high school and college, he always said

the last thing he would ever want was to be married or to have kids."

"He's older now. I'm sure he's changed his mind."

"He dates all the time." She made a face. "I know that. Sometimes he brings women in for cupcakes."

"Oh," I said. "Yeah, forget him. He's an asshole. You can do better than that."

"Thanks, Jules," she said with a sad sort of sigh. "Maybe I'll try online dating after I learn from your tips."

"My tips?" I said and then groaned. "Oh shit, I already forgot what this article was meant to be about. That's it, I really have to focus." I jumped up and ran to the living room, grabbed my bag and headed back to the kitchen. I gave Betsy my phone and took out a pen and my legal pad to start making notes.

"Okay, you start swiping on Tinder and I'm going to start making some notes for some ideas." I wrote Dating Tips on the top of the pad. "Malcolm said he wants the first article up next week, so that means I need to go on a date sometime this week." I rubbed my forehead. "I'm so not ready for this." I groaned, but Betsy just stared at me with a huge smile.

"I'm so ready," she said. "I'm so so ready."

❦ 8 ❦

"Heathcliff, slow down." I gasped as I watched my dog leaping through the sand ahead of me. I pulled on his leash but that had the opposite effect of what I'd been hoping for. He started running faster and I could feel my legs starting to buckle out from under me as I struggled to keep up. "Heathcliff, stop," I screeched finally getting his attention. He stopped abruptly, and the suddenness was too much for my limbs and I went flying to the ground. "Heathcliff." I groaned as he jumped into my lap and started licking my face as I sat up, sand all over my body. "Not cool, Heathcliff." I glared at him, but he just continued licking my face.

"Wow, you found true love fast." I heard Nolan's voice behind me and I stifled a groan. Of course, he would witness my failure at exercise.

"Better than being with someone like you," I said as I turned around and my heart immediately froze as I saw him standing next to some beautiful blonde that was wearing only a bikini. What the hell?

"You okay?" Nolan grinned down at me as he offered me his hand to get back up.

"I'm fine," I said as I ignored his hand and tried to jump back up. "Heathcliff was just being crazy." I stood up and pulled on Heathcliff's leash to bring him closer to me as he had just recognized Nolan and was starting to get excited.

"Heathcliff is her crazy dog," Nolan said to the hot blonde next to him and I wondered exactly how they knew each other. "Ellen, this is Julia, Julia this is Ellen, she just got done playing a beach volleyball match."

"Oh, okay, cool, hi," I said, sounding more awkward than I had ever sounded before in my life.

"Hi, Julia, cute dog," Ellen said with one of those dazzling smiles that made her look even more beautiful but didn't really reach her eyes. She looked me over and I could see from the look in her eyes, she wasn't impressed or worried about me being any sort of competition. "Are we going to go back to my place before dinner, babe?" Ellen looked up at Nolan. "I'm getting a bit cold."

"Sure," Nolan said easily and I could feel my brain going into overdrive. Was Nolan dating Julia? How was that possible? Hadn't he said he wasn't dating and that he was concentrating on work?

"What are you up to tonight, Jules?" Nolan asked me with an easy smile that made me want to smack him. He knew I had no plans.

"Going to see if I have any connections, start getting my dates lined up."

"Dates?" Ellen looked at me curiously. "Oh?"

"Jules just joined some online dating sites."

"Oh." Ellen gave me a dismissive look. "I never use dating sites, I find that only los... I mean, those that find it hard to meet men resort to dating sites."

"We all can't go running around in our bikini's all day trying to impress men," I said before I could stop myself.

"Jules." Nolan shook his head at me, but I could see his eyes sparkling. He was loving this. Asshole!

"Nolan, I'm getting hungry. Can we stop at your sister's bakery before you go to the post office?"

"Sure." He nodded and I watched as they smiled at each other for a few seconds before I realized I was going to puke if I had to watch them much longer.

"Anyway, I have to go. See ya." I grabbed Heathcliff's leash and pulled it and started running again. Heathcliff was more than happy to get going and once again he was sprinting down the beach. I huffed and puffed as I attempted to keep up with him, but I didn't try to slow him down this time. I needed to be winded in order to stop thinking about Nolan and bitchy-ass Ellen. I wanted to call Betsy to find out what she knew about Ellen, but I didn't want her to think I was interested. The last thing I needed was another complication with Nolan.

I HAD RECEIVED FIVE MESSAGES FROM DIFFERENT GUYS ON Tinder. Two of them asked me if I wanted to meet up at a bar that night and hook up. Another one asked me if I was interested in a polyamorous relationship and I just rolled my eyes. The other two guys seemed cool though. The first one's name was Harry, he had dark hair and I couldn't tell what color eyes he had. His message stated that he liked Clint Eastwood movies and kayaking. The second guy said his name was JR and that he was originally from Texas. He looked really tall and built in his photos. He looked like a surfer dude, with light blond hair and big blue eyes. He stated that he loved the water and had just recently moved to Canyon Beach.

I was very happy to note that I'd never met either of these

guys before. I decided to check out my Bumble messages next before I responded to either of the guys. I had matched with twenty guys on Bumble and sent them all a standard, "Hey, how's it going" first message as women had to message first on Bumble. I had six responses to my messages. Three just responded with "hi," but the other three had sent me long messages in response and they seemed really interested in getting to know me. The first guy was "Calvin," he was from Atlanta originally, had been in the Army and now worked as an engineer. He reminded me of a younger-looking Denzel Washington and I had to stop myself from putting that in my response. I was sure he had heard that a million times.

The next guy was called, "Stuart," and while he seemed friendly in his message, I just couldn't get past the fact that he stated he loved Pokémon. I mean, I wasn't the most mature of women, but I just wasn't on board with dating a guy that was into Pokémon.

The last guy was Jose, and he was the most handsome of all the men that had messaged me so far. In fact, he was so handsome, that I was shocked he had matched with me. He didn't look super tall, but he had jet-black hair, big deep brown eyes, a dark bronze complexion and a wide grin that showed off his perfect white teeth and luscious pink lips. He hadn't said anything about himself other than the fact that he was from Central America and was into cooking. I wondered if he knew how to make empanadas. They were one of my favorite foods, but I wasn't about to ask him that right away.

"What's cooking, good-looking?" Stella answered the phone in her singsong voice and I laughed.

"Okay, two things. I have some hot guys who have messaged me, how do I respond letting them know I want a date without sounding desperate?"

"And?"

"And I saw Nolan on a date with some fake blonde ho."

"A professional ho?"

"No." I laughed. "I'm just being a hater. She was some gorgeous model type, and she was in her bikini with her awesome *Sports Illustrated* body and she was going to dinner with Nolan and she was just so fake and plastic."

"You seem to know her well."

"As well as you can know someone in one minute." I giggled.

"You so love him."

"No, I don't," I protested. "I love Jose."

"Who?" Stella sounded confused.

"Jose, one of my potential dates from Bumble."

"He won't be a date if he thinks you love him already. I don't know everything about guys but I know the *L* word too soon is a relationship killer."

"Ha ha, I love you, Stella."

"I love you too. First things first, be straight up, say something like, I think you seem cool and I prefer to meet in person as soon as possible so as not to waste time, what do you think? And most guys will be happy with that. Second thing, if you like Nolan, you should let him know."

"I don't like him," I said quickly. "It was just awkward."

"Me thinks you have never forgotten that first kiss."

"Trust me, I have," I lied. "I can't even remember what it was like."

"Uh-huh, so tell me more about Jose and these other guys."

"Oh, there was one guy that asked if I was into polyamorous relationships, like yeah right, no thanks."

"Wait," Stella said. "I think you should meet him."

"What?" I shouted into the phone. "Are you joking?"

"No, hear me out. Think about it. This is for your articles, right? Readers want to know about all sorts of crazy and different dates. Remember, you're not going on dates just for you, you're going on dates to inform readers of dating tips. There might be readers out there that are interested in open relationships."

"Ugh, why would anyone want to be in an open relationship?"

"I don't know, but that's the sort of information that you will be able to gather on your date, right?"

"You're right." I sighed. "I will message him back."

"Good. I can't wait to read all about it."

"Uh-huh." I laughed. "Okay, I'm going to go now. I need to respond to these guys and do some more swiping."

"Sounds good. Speak to you later, doll."

"Bye, Stella. Sweet dreams." I hung up the phone and got ready to start responding to the messages. I was just about to put my phone away when I decided to do a couple more swipes. I needed to up my connections so that I could have more potential dates. And just as I was about to put my phone away again, there he appeared, Lucas Sacramento in the flesh. His beaming face filled up my screen and I could hear myself squealing. He looked absolutely gorgeous. The young, tall geeky boy had grown up and was now super built and hot as hell. His bright blue eyes dazzled in his tan face and his hair was now slightly too long and wavy. He was on the beach in his profile photo and only wearing white swim trunks that showed off his perfect chest and studly legs. I whistled as I clicked through the rest of his photos. This guy was hot. I couldn't believe that his wife had cheated on him. I swiped right and was overjoyed to see that we matched immediately. That meant he had already seen my photo and swiped right as well. That meant that he was interested in me and how I looked now. I tried to stifle my excitement, but I couldn't. I jumped up and called out to Heathcliff, he came running and I attempted to dance around the room with him. I couldn't wait to see what Lucas was going to write to me in the app. I just couldn't wait. I ignored the fact that it was Nolan's face that popped into my head as I brushed my teeth and got ready for bed.

❦ 9 ❦

To: CreativewriterJules
   From: ThirdbaseJose

HEY GIRL, LOOKING CUTE. HOW'S YOUR WEEK GOING?
What's your name?

JOSE

To: THIRDBASEJOSE
   From: CreativewriterJules

HI JOSE,
   My name is Julia. Pretty great. ~~Now I'm talking to you~~.
How are you? What does your screen name mean? ~~A sexual
reference or baseball~~? It's very unique. Do you enjoy cooking?

. . .

JULES

TO: CREATIVEWRITERJULES
    From: ThirdbaseJose

JULIA,
    What do you think my name means? ;)
    Cooking? Sometimes. Do you cook? Offering to make me dinner?
    Any plans this weekend?

JOSE

TO: THIRDBASEJOSE
    From: CreativewriterJules

HEY JOSE,
    I think it means you're good at baseball. I'm not the best cook, though my friend Betsy is amazing. ~~Do you make empanadas? Are you from Argentina?~~ Where are you from originally? Just curious as to what sort of cuisine you might make. No plans for this weekend? ~~What about you? Want to ask me on a date?~~ Is it okay if everything gets recorded?

JULES

TO: CREATIVEWRITERJULES

From: ThirdbaseJose

JULIA,

What do you mean where am I from? I'm American! Is it because I look Latin?

JK, I'm originally from Mexico. At least that's what my parents tell me. They're from Guadalajara. Have you heard of it? Maybe if this works out we can go to Cancun or something and rent a private villa? Wanna grab a drink on Friday night!

JOSE

TO: THIRDBASEJOSE
From: CreativewriterJules

JOSE,

PLEASE FORGIVE ME FOR MY FAUX PAS. I DIDN'T MEAN TO assume or say that you weren't American! I'd love a drink on Friday night! Where shall we meet? ~~Don't think we're going to be renting a private villa but whatevs~~.

JULES

I GRABBED MY PHONE AND SENT A TEXT TO STELLA, BETSY, and Nolan with the same message. "Holla, guess who just landed their first date? This *chica* here." I hit send and sat back at my desk with a smile. I could already tell that Third-base Jose was not going to be the guy for me, but it was nice to have a date lined up already. It felt a little bit exciting, even though I knew it wasn't really a real date. He wasn't going to become my true love or anything. However, Jose was hot. He had updated his profile with some new photographs and I just couldn't stop myself from smiling and pinching myself. I couldn't believe that such a hottie wanted to take me out. Not that I was grotesque. I was pretty enough, but I wasn't a Hollywood beauty by any means and this guy looked like a better looking Enrique Iglesias. Even if he was interested, I was still waiting to hear from Lucas on the app. I was actually surprised that he hadn't messaged me already, but figured that he was just really shy.

"Tell me all," Betsy sang into the phone as soon as I picked up. "What's his name? Age? Also, send me some photos."

"Betsy." I laughed. "You know this is for a job, right?"

"I know." She giggled. "I'm just so excited for you. It's Jules, Grandma Elsie, she just got a date so I'm asking her about it. Sorry," she said into the phone. "Grandma Elsie is helping out at the bakery today and heard me on the phone."

"No worries." I heard a beep on my phone and saw Nolan was calling me. "Hey, I have to go, your brother is on the other line."

"Oh Nolan." Betsy groaned. "He's always there. Nolan is calling Jules right now, Grandma, not me." She laughed as her grandma said something in the background. "I don't know, Grandma. Hey Jules, I'll let you go. Call me back later, okay?"

"Okay, bye," I said and clicked over to the other call. "Goodburger, home of the Goodburger, can I take your order?"

"Very funny, Jules." Nolan's voice was dry. "So you have a date already?"

"Surprised?"

"No," he said and laughed slightly.

"Jealous?"

"Not quite. I'm just wondering if you and Malcolm had figured out how legally you were going to take me along and have me taking photos and videos of the two of you."

"Oh," I said and blinked. "I don't know. I didn't even think about it. I thought you guys had it all figured out."

"If you guys want to use these images, you will need permission from your dates. You guys don't want to get sued."

"This wasn't even my idea." My voice rose.

"Well, I know you're all excited about your date and all, but maybe you need to be thinking responsibly as well."

"Excuse me?" My voice grew even louder. "I am responsible."

"You could have fooled me." His voice sounded confident and it angered me even more.

"Oh shut up, Nolan," I said annoyed. "What do you want?"

"I just told you."

"Was that all?"

"Yes," he said and then I hung up on him. Like really? He was the one that had initially communicated with Malcolm, not me. So why was it me that was now in charge of making sure we legally recorded my dates. I sighed as I stood up and walked to Malcolm's office. Even though it annoyed me, I knew Nolan was right. There was no way we could secretly record my dates. I just didn't know what sort of guy would be genuine and real if he knew he was being recorded.

"Malcolm, do you have a second?" I said as I knocked on his door. He looked up from his computer screen with a small frown on his face.

"Sure, Julia, what's going on?" He ushered me into his office and I sat in the chair across from him.

"Legally we can't just video and photograph my dates. There's no way we can get away with that."

"Okay." He nodded. "And?"

"And, so what's the plan?" I asked him, keeping my voice in check as he was annoying me as well.

"The plan?" He shrugged. "I guess tell them and ask them after the date?"

"That's not really a good plan. What if they say no?" I said after a few seconds.

"Well, tell them beforehand?" His eyes flickered back to his screen and I could tell that he wasn't really paying attention to me.

"Is everything okay, Malcolm?" I asked him, starting to feel concerned about his behavior. This wasn't like him.

"What?" He gazed at me as if he had no idea what I'd just said. "Oh yes, yes, yes, everything is fine."

"Um okay."

"Go to Jackson Mclintock, our attorney to work out an agreement for your dates to sign," Malcolm said after a few seconds. "Make sure to have them sign the contract before the date and we should be fine."

"But how am I supposed to tell them?" I made a face. "And what if they change the way they act because they know they're being recorded?"

"You'll figure it out, Julia." He heaved a big sigh. "I have to make a call. Anything else?"

"No." I shook my head and stood up. "I'll go and chat with Jackson Mclintock now, if that's okay?"

"Sure." He smiled at me. "Tell him I said hello."

"Okay," I said and walked out of his office. That had been a really weird conversation. Malcolm was never that out of it. He must be really stressed out about how the newspaper was doing. I walked back to my desk and then looked online for Jackson's phone number. Jackson Mclintock was well known in town, for having been the star quarterback of the high school football team and the mayor's son and I also knew of him because he was one of Nolan's old friends.

"Good day, this is the law office of Mclintock and Holmes, how may I direct your call?" a perky voice answered the phone.

"May I speak to Jackson, please?"

"Who shall I say is calling?"

"Julia Gilbert."

"Jules?" Her voice suddenly changed and lost all professionalism. "It's me, Emily. Emily Lutz."

"Emily?"

"From AP English?"

"Oh yeah, yeah. How are you?" I asked, vaguely remembering a cute redhead that always talked about her love for young adult books, like *Sweet Valley Twins*, even though we were seniors in high school.

"Oh, just great. Working for Jackson Mclintock." She sighed dreamily. "I can't believe my luck."

"Are you an attorney?" I asked surprised. When we were in school, she'd always said she wanted to be an actress or singer.

"No." She laughed. "I'm the head receptionist here at the firm. Jackson has a lot of faith in me."

"Oh wow, how many receptionists does he have?" I asked surprised. How many calls could he be getting each day? It wasn't like our town was very big.

"Just me." She giggled. "But it's such an honor working for him, he's so smart and handsome, and..." Her voice trailed off and she giggled again. I rolled my eyes as I sat on the other side of the phone. So she was definitely still an airhead then.

"Sorry to interrupt you, Emily, but is Jackson there? I'm

working at the *Canyon Beach Chronicle* now and he's our attorney and we have an urgent question for him."

"Oh, of course," she said sweetly. "I thought you might have been one of his admirers trying to get through, but if it's for the paper, of course. I'll put you through now."

"Thanks, Emily."

"Bye, Jules," she said and I then found myself listening to the boring wait music that companies play to make you hang up the phone.

"Julia Gilbert," A smooth deep voice answered the phone. "Is that you?"

"Hi, Jackson, yes, it's me."

"Well, how's that for a good day?" he said, with a small chuckle. "You know I was just thinking about you the other day."

"You were?" I asked surprised. I didn't think that Jackson Mclintock had ever really noticed me.

"Yes, do you remember that weekend that Nolan and I visited you in college?"

"Uh..." My voice stalled as my face reddened. I never wanted to think about that weekend again, in my life.

"You and that guy you were dating had just broken up remember and Nolan had that copy of *Pride and Prejudice* that he gave you?"

"Yeah, I vaguely remember, why?"

"Oh." He laughed. "I met a girl in your dorm and we had some fun that weekend and I was trying to remember her name and I was going to call and ask you."

"Oh," I said and then shook my head to myself. He was still a pig then. "Hey Jackson, I'm actually calling on official newspaper business," I hurriedly explained to him what we were after and I waited for him to respond.

"I see... hmm... so you're dating up a storm now?"

"I wouldn't say that. It's for work."

"I can send you out a contract that you can have the guys sign before the dates start."

"So I have to have them do that?"

"Yes." His voice was serious now. "You will put the paper in legal jeopardy if you don't have them sign this paper before any photos are taken." He cleared his throat. "Malcolm can't afford to get sued for anything right now."

"Well, the articles were his idea," I said defensively, but his words made me pause. Did everyone know that the paper wasn't doing well? Maybe it was a lot more serious than I'd originally thought. What if I lost my job? I swallowed hard as I realized that it wasn't only the *Canyon Beach Chronicle* that needed for this series of articles to really take off. I needed it to do well myself.

10

"Aww, he is just too sweet and perfect," I said to Heathcliff as I reread the latest letter I'd received from Fitz. I was still surprised that Lucas hadn't messaged me on the dating app as yet, but I figured that he was more comfortable with the letter writing.

Dearest Julia,

My schedule is quite busy at the moment but I would love to meet eventually. I hope you don't mind us writing for the time being. I'm sure you have many questions, but for now, let's just get to know each other. Have you read any good books recently? I seem to recall that you loved books. Do you still read a lot? I recently read a book called "A Man Called Ove," by Fredrik Backman and it was really heartfelt and touching. I think you would enjoy it. Do you still love Jane Austen as much as you did in high school?

Yours,

Fitz

I put the letter back down and smiled to myself as I decided to wait to respond to his letter. I didn't want him to think I was too eager. Heathcliff was curled up at my feet and I had a light cotton blanket over my lap as I lay back on the couch and watched TV. I had recently become obsessed with a show called *The Bold Type* and I had been watching the episodes since I'd gotten off of work. "Oh Sutton," I groaned as she gave her boyfriend, Richard, another dismissal. "What are you doing?" I saw Heathcliff looking at me curiously and laughed at the puzzled expression in his brown eyes. He had no idea who I was talking to. "I'm not going crazy, Heathcliff, don't worry," I said as the doorbell rang. I sat up and frowned, the puzzled expression now on my face. I had no idea who could be at my door. I got up and walked to my front door and turned on the corridor light?

"Hello," I said as I opened the door and a wave of surprise crashed over me as I saw Nolan standing there with a bottle of wine in one hand and a bag in the other. "What are you doing here?"

"It's nice to see you as well, Jules," he said with a small grin as he held up the wine bottle. "Can I come in?"

"Um, why?" I said not shifting.

"I realized that I was too harsh with you about the contract for your dates. It's not on you. I wanted to apologize and see if we can figure out a way to ensure your dates don't run when they see me with the camera."

"You want to help me?" I asked him, my voice expressing my shock. "And you brought wine? For me?"

"Well, for us." He winked. "Can I come in?"

"Sure," I said and stepped back. He looked me over in my skimpy tank top and shorts and I suddenly felt severely underdressed as his smile grew. He looked at me and I waited for him to tease me or make fun of me. "Nothing to say?" I asked him as he followed me to the living room and he just shook his head.

"Hey, Heathcliff." He scratched Heathcliff behind the ears as the dog beamed up at him, tail wagging. "How's my favorite dog?" He grinned, and I just shook my head.

"Don't encourage him." I sat down on the couch and pressed pause on the TV. "So what's going on?"

"Can we open this wine before we start talking?" He held up the bottle again and shook it around a little bit.

"I thought you preferred beer."

"I do, but I brought wine for you and I don't want you to have to drink it alone."

"What if I don't want to drink any right now?"

"You're turning down a drink?"

"I'm not a lush, you know."

"I know that, Jules," he said as he walked closer to me, his eyes sparkling. He stopped right in front of me and stared into my eyes for a good minute or so.

"What are you doing?" I swallowed hard as I stared up at him. He was too good-looking and he knew it.

"I wasn't aware that I was doing anything." He winked at me and my heart fluttered as he reached over and brushed a stray hair from my face. "Your hair is growing so long again."

"Yeah, I decided to grow it out again. Didn't love it short," I remarked on his comment. I'd had long hair almost all of my life, but right after college graduation, I had decided to cut it into a bob. It hadn't suited my face and I had been praying desperately for it to grow back out. "Let me go and get a corkscrew." I almost ran away from him as his finger traced a line down my cheek toward my mouth. "And uh, two glasses."

"Oh and a plate. Grandma Elsie gave me some brownies to bring."

"Oh?" I stopped at the doorway and looked back at him. "She did?"

"Yeah, she knew I was going to come over tonight." He held up a white bag. "We all know how much you love your sweets."

"Yes, we do." I laughed. "Hold on, I'll be right back." I

hurried to the kitchen and then back to the living room. "Make yourself at home," I said sarcastically as I stared at him sitting on the couch with Heathcliff in his lap. "Heathcliff, you are a fair-weather dog."

"Aww, you'll hurt his feelings, just like you hurt mine." Nolan made a sad face, and I laughed.

"As if." I placed the glasses on the table and handed him the corkscrew. "Wine please." I sat on the couch next to him and watched as he started opening the bottle. "It's nice of you to grow a conscience, but I spoke to Jackson today and we're going to just give the guys a contract to sign."

"Yes, but do you know how you're going to bring it up?" he asked me with a curious expression on his face. I could tell from the look in his eyes that he knew that I had no idea what I was going to say.

"Not quite." I made a face and sighed. "I mean who in their right mind would want to go on a date after someone asked them if they would sign a contract. Someone they've never even met, to boot."

"Well, I think you'd be surprised." He handed me a glass. "I actually think that you should include the fact that you're a journalist into your profile."

"Really? Why?"

"Because you can casually mention that you decided to combine your love of writing and dating and say that you're getting paid to date. Trust me, most men will be okay with that."

"Would you be okay with that?" I stared into his eyes.

"If the date was with you, then maybe..." He grinned.

"Yeah right." I rolled my eyes and took a huge gulp of wine.

"I was going to say maybe not, but you interrupted me."

"Why are you so mean to me?" I moved away from him on the couch, upset that he had dissed me in that way.

"Sorry, I really don't mean to be, but when I'm around you I'm taken back to my teenage years and having to look after you and Betsy."

"You never had to look after me and Betsy." I shook my head. "What sort of revisionist history is that?"

"Well, you know what I mean? I can remember you as a preteen. Sometimes it's hard to forget," he said and then his eyes gazed over my body.

"You weren't exactly an old man, Nolan. You're only a few years older than me."

"Well, it sure felt like a lot back then."

"Back when?" I watched as he moved closer to me on the couch and I found myself glued to my spot. What was he doing?

"Back in the days you were trying to kiss me all the time," he said slowly and I watched as he took a sip of his wine.

"There were never any days where I was trying to kiss you all the time," I mumbled, blushing.

"You don't remember sneaking to my room one night wanting to do more than kiss?" he said, a wide grin on his face as his eyes laughed at me. "I seem to remember that."

"I thought you were here to talk about work and my dates." I moved away from him on the couch feeling flustered. Why was he bringing all of this up now?

"You asked me a question, and I answered it. I always wonder what would have happened that night if I hadn't said no."

"Nothing would have happened. I was just testing you."

"Were you testing me in college as well?"

"Nolan." I groaned, starting to feel annoyed. "Why are you bringing this up?"

"No reason." His eyes moved to my heaving chest and I could feel my nipples hardening under his gaze. "I see you gave up the cartoon character pj's."

"I'm not a kid anymore."

"I can see that." He put his glass down and I felt his hand on my thigh, lightly resting there as if that were the most natural place in the world for it to be. My heart was racing, and I was excited to find out what he was going to do next. I knew I should have hit his hand away, but I didn't want him to move it. "You were always beautiful though," he said as he leaned in toward me and my entire body stilled as I waited for him to kiss me.

"What?" I said after he just stared at me without doing a thing. Was he expecting me to lean forward and kiss him?

"Was just wondering if you needed any more lessons."

"Lessons?"

"Kissing lessons," he said and before I knew it, his lips were on mine and he was kissing me. At first, his lips felt tender against mine and then, then they were more pressing, more demanding. As his tongue slipped into my mouth, I knew that he wanted more from me. He wanted me to kiss him back, to submit to him. His fingers stroked my naked thigh, and I knew that I could no longer just sit there, not reacting or touching him. My lips moved against his as my tongue linked with his and I grabbed his hair, running my hand through his silky tresses. He groaned against my lips and I felt his hand sliding up my thigh and then to my neck, pulling me closer to him. We fell back on the couch and Heathcliff gave a little yelp and jumped off, the action making us draw apart momentarily to laugh. We laughed for a few seconds and then Nolan growled and pulled my face back down to his and kissed me harder. His hands ran down my back and toward my ass. I felt his fingers on the back of my thighs and then inside my thighs and my breathing grew harder. I writhed against him, feeling turned on and I kissed him back passionately. My breasts were crushed against his chest and I reached my hand up under his T-shirt to feel his bare skin. His skin felt warm and smooth and muscular and I loved feeling his heartbeat racing under my touch. He growled and rolled me over gently on the couch so that we were facing each other. He pulled his T-shirt off and threw it onto the ground and then he started to pull my tank top off. I lifted my arms up so that he could pull it all the way off of me. I was now lying there in my pink bra and shorts, but to my sadness he didn't take off my bra. Instead, he slid the straps off of my shoulders and pulled them down slightly. With his eyes still on mine, he moved forward and kissed all over my breast, carefully avoiding my nipple. I was still as I waited to feel his lips on me more intimately and when his lips finally made contact with my nipple and his teeth lightly tugged on my sensitive spot, I cried out in shock and excited surprise.

"Like that, do you?" He grinned and before I could respond he was kissing me again and this time his fingers were caressing my breasts, brushing over my nipples back and forth. I trembled slightly as we kissed and I ran my hands to his hair. He kissed down my neck and his fingers ran up and down my inner thighs moving closer and closer to my sweet spot. He pushed my thighs apart slightly and I gasped as he rubbed in between my legs. His eyes stared into mine and they seemed to be laughing at me as I kissed him back hard. My whole body was on fire and I felt like I was flying through the sky as his fingers slipped into my panties. I moaned, and he kissed me harder. I couldn't believe this was happening. I had always dreamed of being this intimate with Nolan but hadn't thought it would ever happen after everything that had happened in college.

"You're so wet, already." He grunted against my lips. I reached down and rubbed the front of his jeans and I could feel that he was hard already. I laughed slightly as I felt his cock move beneath my fingers. It seemed to be growing harder and larger as I rubbed and all I wanted was to see it naked and proud in front of me. I felt his mouth moving back down to my breast and I was about to go to unbuckle his jeans when the doorbell rang. We both stopped what we were doing and he looked at me quizzically.

"Expecting someone?"

"No." I shook my head as the doorbell rang again. "I have no idea who that could be." I got up off of the couch slowly, feeling slightly dazed. Nolan jumped up beside me and pulled my bra straps up before handing me my tank top. "Here you go," he said with a grin and I pulled it on quickly before heading to the front door.

"Hey, Jackson," I said, surprised to see the attorney in front of me. "What are you doing here?"

"Sorry for just stopping over, but I thought I could deliver the contract directly to you and just pop by and say hi."

"Hi," I said, slightly taken aback by his huge grin. Jackson was tall at six four with golden-blond hair and big blue eyes. He looked like the typical all-American boy and had been super popular in high school and college. Unlike most good-looking high school athletes, he had aged well, and I was surprised at the flirtatious look on his face.

"Can I come in?" he asked, stepping into my foyer without waiting for a response.

"Jackson?" Nolan walked out of the living room with his shirt still off and I blushed as Jackson gave me a shocked look with a huge grin.

"Well, I'll be." He walked over to Nolan and held up his hand for a high five. "Nolan Montgomery, what are you doing here, you old dog you?"

"Hanging out with Jules," Nolan said dryly. "What are you doing here?" His eyes narrowed as he stared at Jackson and he certainly didn't share the same wide-mouthed grin that Jackson was wearing on his face.

"Just came to drop off the contract Jules needs for her dating article. I hear you're going to be the photographer." He cocked his head at Nolan. "Or are you going to be more?"

"More?"

"Another coach?" He winked and then laughed and went for a fist bump, but Nolan just glared at him.

"Coach?" I asked, my face reddening. What was he talking about?

"Like in high school, when he had to teach you how to kiss for your play."

"He told you about that?" I asked, my face burning with shame.

"He told all of us." Jackson laughed. "Boy, that was priceless, eh, Nolan."

"Leave the contract and go please, Jackson." Nolan looked annoyed.

"Sure." Jackson grinned as he handed me the contract. "How's Ellen, by the way? Heard you guys were going out now."

"Heard from who?" Nolan's expression became cold.

"This is a small town, Nolan." Jackson shrugged. "It was good seeing you, Jules. Maybe you'll let me take you out on one of your dates."

"Maybe." I smiled back at him weakly. "Thanks for getting me the contract."

"No worries. I'll give you a call." He nodded at me and then turned to Nolan. "See you around, dude."

"See ya," Nolan said and walked Jackson to the front door. As soon as Jackson walked out, he slammed the door behind him. "Before you say anything, let me explain," he said as soon as he turned around to face me.

"Explain what?" I glared at him. "The fact that you made fun of me to your high school buddies."

"I didn't make fun of you."

"Did you tell them about the other nights as well?" I wanted to cry, I felt so embarrassed.

"No, no, of course not. I was out of high school then. I regretted ever telling anyone about that first night." He walked toward me and put his hands on my arms. "I know you're upset at me."

"I'm not upset," I lied and averted my gaze from his eyes.

"Can I kiss you?" he asked as he moved closer to me, his lips trying to find mine.

"Nope," I said and pulled away from him.

"Then I think you're lying to me about being upset," he said with a sigh. "Jules, that was years ago."

"I'm not upset. I just don't think we should be kissing right now. It's not appropriate," I said and looked at him with a haughty look. "I'm about to start writing an article about dating and meeting my true love. I don't need to be knocking boots with you."

"Knocking boots?" He burst out laughing. "Do you mean having sex?"

"You know what I mean." I glared at him.

"So we were going to have sex?"

"Nolan!" I groaned and folded my arms. "You should leave."

"But I haven't finished..."

"Nolan." I gasped. "That's so crude."

"I was going to say I haven't finished drinking my wine. Get your mind out of the gutter, Jules. Really?"

"Ugh, you're so frustrating." I marched back to the living room. "I can't believe I was just kissing you."

"We were doing more than kissing," he said following me. "Can I sleep over tonight?"

"What?" My jaw dropped and I blinked at him as I turned around. "You what?"

"Well, I've been drinking and you know I don't like to drink and drive."

"Nolan Montgomery, you haven't even had one glass of wine." I shook my head at him as he burst out laughing. "And there is a company known as Uber, you know?"

"I don't want to be kidnapped," he said in a deadpan voice and then it was my turn to start laughing.

"You're totally ridiculous, you know that, right?"

"Would you want me any other way?" he asked with a boyish grin and I could feel my heart racing at his goofy smile. I couldn't believe that I still had a soft spot for him. "So are you looking forward to your first date?"

"That's a weird question to ask me after just trying to kiss me."

"Touché," he said as he sat back down on the couch. "Shall we watch a movie?"

"You're staying?"

He nodded and raised his wineglass. "Unless you're kicking me out."

"No, but I do need to do some work before we watch anything."

"Work?" He raised an eyebrow. "Finishing off an article?"

"No, I need to do some swiping and responding to some messages."

"Oh, hmm." He sat back. "You have to do that tonight?"

"If I want enough dates to write these articles then yes."

"Fine, go ahead." He grabbed the remote control. "Don't forget to update your profile and say you're a journalist as well."

"Yes, boss," I said as I grabbed my laptop and my phone and sat back down on the couch next to him. "Anything else?" I asked him mockingly.

"Yeah..." He leaned toward me. "Can I get another kiss before you get to work?"

"Are you serious?" I couldn't tell if he was teasing me or if he really wanted another kiss.

"Nope." He grinned as he powered through the TV channels.

"So what's going on with you and Ellen?" I asked casually as I opened my laptop. I didn't want him to think that I cared, so I didn't look at him as I waited for his answer.

"Not much. We're just casually going on some dates," he said smoothly, and I wanted to scream. What the hell did that mean? Were they sleeping together? The thought made my stomach curdle. Was he in love with her? The thought made my heart ache. And even worse, if he was dating her, what the hell was he doing here with me? Of course, I didn't ask him any of those questions. I wasn't absolutely pathetic, and I knew what Nolan wanted. He was just about fun. He never stayed in a relationship longer than a few months. There was no point in me asking him more questions about Ellen or trying to figure out if he actually liked me. He hadn't said anything about taking me on a date or wanting to be in a relationship with me. All he had done was kiss me and ask to sleep over. I knew what he wanted and it would only make our relationship even more awkward if I asked him deep questions that were not appropriate for our relationship; whatever it was. "What's going on with you and Jackson?"

"Me and Jackson?" I asked him with a small frown. "What are you talking about? There's nothing going on with me and Jackson."

"He just decided to show up at your house tonight because..." His voice trailed off and his eyes searched mine.

"You just showed up at my house tonight as well," I said pointedly.

"But you're best friends with my sister and well, you know." He shrugged.

"No, I know what?"

"You know?"

"Nope."

"We're..." He paused for a few seconds and then smiled. "We're working together."

"Okay, Nolan. Whatever you say." I logged into my email account and decided to ignore him. I had no idea what Nolan wanted from me, but after the incident in college, I was done with trying to get closer to him. He'd embarrassed me too many times before. I heard a beeping on my phone and looked down to see a notification that Jose had just sent me a message. "Speak of the devil," I said with a smile as I opened the message.

"Who's that?" Nolan leaned over and scowled as he looked down at my phone screen.

"Jose, my first date."

"Jose, huh?" His lips thinned. "Any photos?"

"Yes." I opened his profile, proud to show off how handsome he looked.

"These look fake," Nolan said in a tight voice. "He looks like he stole them from IMDB."

"What?"

"I bet he's some sort of famous actor in Latin America."

"He's American and his parents are from Mexico, actually."

"Hmm." He looked into my eyes. "If you say so."

"That's him," I said with confidence, even though I really had no idea.

"You always did like tall, dark, and handsome."

"Excuse me?"

"Well, you wanted me as well." He laughed and I pushed his shoulder lightly. He grabbed my hand and pulled me toward him so that I was slightly on his lap. "Didn't you?"

"No," I lied as I looked up at him. "Nolan, I need to work."

"So you can consider Jose work?" he said with a huge grin and I just rolled my eyes at him as I pulled away from him and read my latest message from Jose.

"Good evening, Jules. I'm very excited to meet you for drinks. I keep looking at your photos and I have to admit that you're my dream girl. I was wondering if you enjoy kissing on the first date. Your Prince Charming, Jose." I ignored the silent laughter that was coming from Nolan as I finished reading and starting writing my response.

"You're seriously going to go on a date with that guy?" He chuckled. "Should I start calling you, Princess Julia?"

"Yes, plebe."

"Do you want me to start bowing to you now or can I wait until it's official?"

"Nolan Montgomery, you are so immature. I can't believe that you're almost thirty."

"Well, believe it." He winked at me. "I can do things that only men my age can do."

"What sort of things?" I said and then groaned as I realized I'd walked right into that one. "You know what, don't answer me." I made a face at him and started typing and explaining to Jose that I was a journalist. To be fair, his message had turned me off, but I wasn't going to admit that to Nolan. Plus, it was only one date. It wasn't like I had to marry the guy. I just hoped that I would connect with some nice guys. I was ready to start dating again and wanted to find someone as soon as possible before I became hung up on Nolan again. That was a time of my life that I didn't want to relive.

11

Q ueen of First Dates by Julia Montgomery
The First Date

HELLO READERS, MY NAME IS JULIA AND I HOPE YOU'RE READY to follow me on my dating journey. Dating has always been an exciting part of most people's lives, yet in this day and age, the process of dating has really changed. My weekly articles will be here to try to help you navigate the process of online dating. I'm no expert, but hopefully, we will both learn on our journey together. Normally, in online articles and books, names are changed to protect the privacy of the people named, but to ensure these articles are transparent, real names and photographs will be used. I want you to be able to relate and trust me on this journey. Wish me luck. And without further ado, let me introduce you to Jose, my first date. My first piece of advice is to set boundaries from the beginning, otherwise, your date might take things down a path you're not willing to go. And always remember that good-looking doesn't always equal good...

. . .

Thanks to the Canyon Beach Flower Shop for sponsoring this first date.

I SHOULD HAVE KNOWN WHEN JOSE GAVE ME A LONG slightly too intimate hug as soon as he met me and started talking to me in Spanish that something was amiss, but I dismissed the warning bells in my head because he was even more handsome than he'd looked in his photos.

"*Hola, mi preciosa Julia, eres más linda en persona que en tus fotos. Y tu cuerpo está encendido. Espero que esta noche podamos divertirnos y no como si estuviéramos jugando juegos de mesa,*" he said smoothly and I just smiled at him not knowing what he was saying as his eyes ran up and down my body.

"Uh, hi, Jose," I said and then he reached down and grabbed my hand and raised it to his lips.

"Sorry, I will speak in English. It is really nice to meet you." When he spoke in English, he had no accent and I wondered if he had been faking his heavy Spanish accent when he'd spoken to me in Spanish. "Is that your photographer?" He nodded over to Nolan who was standing right behind me, a red light shining on the front of his camera, letting me know that he was already taking video. I could already feel myself becoming self-conscious and stopped myself from glaring at him.

"Yes, and thanks for sending me the contract back this morning. I know this is a bit weird," I mumbled almost incoherently, not really knowing what to say.

"Hey, I would have signed anything if it meant I got to go on a date with you," he said smoothly and I could see Nolan rolling his eyes as he filmed us.

"You're too nice." I laughed as he led me toward a table.

"*Coño tu estás tan buena. Como yo deseo sentir tus labios por todo mi cuerpo,*" he said as he stared at my lips.

"Sorry, I don't speak Spanish."

"No worries," he said, but he didn't translate what he'd said. "I can't believe you're still single."

"Oh, thanks I guess."

"You're a woman right?"

"Sorry, what?"

"No judgment, it's cool and all that." He looked me up and down. "And I can tell you're all woman."

"So, Jose, tell me more about yourself."

"What do you want to know?" he said to me, but I could see him looking at the camera, his perfect white teeth shining.

"Is the camera bothering you?" I asked with a sigh. This was never going to work if he was more interested in the camera than he was in me.

"*Cara*," he started, and I held my hand up.

"Can we keep it in English, please?" I asked him with a small smile. "I have to plead my ignorance at not knowing another language. I wish I had been one of those smart enough to have paid attention in school and actually picked up a second language, but I'm afraid I didn't."

"I can teach you all the Spanish you want to know."

"You're a big flirt, aren't you?" I said with a sigh. Okay, there had to be a way to salvage this date. This could not end up as my first date in ages. It didn't even matter that it wasn't officially a real date. This was just plain embarrassing; especially seeing as Nolan was witnessing everything.

"No, I'm not a big flirt." His expression changed and he sat back. "What would you like to drink?"

"Um…" I nibbled on my lower lip. We were at a bar, but I didn't know if it was okay to drink on the job. Shouldn't I have my wits about me? But then, shouldn't I do what I would normally do on a date and night out. "Sure, I'll have a Pear Martini, please."

"Fancy," he said in a very deep American accent and I looked at him with narrowed eyes. "What?" he said as he saw me staring up at him.

"How was your accent so different just now?" I asked him curiously. "Five minutes ago you sounded like..." I paused as I didn't know how to state what I was thinking in a polite way that didn't come across as rude.

"You can say it." He raised an eyebrow at me and I blinked.

"Say what?"

"Five minutes ago, I sounded like you expected me to sound, a heavily accented Mexican."

"I didn't even know you were Mexican until you told me."

"Okay then, a heavily accented Latino."

"Sorry what?" My jaw dropped. "I never expected anything. I was just confused because five minutes ago you were speaking with a deep accent and now you sound like you came from Arkansas."

"I did grow up in the South, we can't help our accents you know." He laughed, and I just stared at him. Was he joking around or was he seriously upset with me?

"I didn't mean to make you feel like I felt like you should have a deep Spanish accent."

"You didn't." He gave me a guilty grin. "Sorry, I was a little peeved when you asked me where I was from and wanted to play a little joke on you, but I forgot you don't know me well enough for that to be funny."

"Oh." I sat back nonplussed. He had a point. I had asked him where he was from. Not because I assumed he wasn't American, but more because I was curious about his heritage, given his darker good looks. As the thought crossed my mind, I immediately realized that even though I hadn't consciously wanted to offend him that I most probably had. "Sorry, I didn't mean to make you feel like I thought you were an immigrant."

"Nothing wrong with being an immigrant," he shot back and I stifled a groan. This was going down a more serious path than I had expected. I wasn't opposed to political discussion and I even had strong feelings on the subject myself, but this wasn't really the time or place for our first serious discussion. "Sorry." He started laughing as he reached forward and grabbed my hand. "I'm just joking. I'm not upset."

"Okay," I said weakly. "I'm an immigrant as well. Well, descendent of immigrants."

"Cool. From where?"

"My dad's parents are from England," I said with a small smile. "Boring."

"Not boring, England is cool."

"Yeah, I think that's why I love Shakespeare so much," I said. "And my mom's parents were quite cool, her mom is from South Carolina, and her ancestors were slaves from Africa and her dad was a Jew from Poland."

"Whoa." His eyes widened. "No way." He looked me up and down. "I never would have guessed."

"Ha ha." I laughed lightly, not feeling offended at all. I knew that most people were surprised at my background when they found out. "I just wanted you to know that I understand what it can feel like when you feel like people are questioning who you are, I didn't want to make you feel uncomfortable or anything."

"This is a pretty deep start to a first date, isn't it?" He looked at me with a really surprised expression. "You're not what I expected."

"Oh?"

"Well, you're so hot I just assumed you were one of the Canyon Beach bimbos that I always meet."

"I'm not a bimbo." I accepted his hot comment and grinned.

"Yeah, you're not."

"And you're way hotter than me," I said with a small laugh, at this point having forgotten that Nolan was in the corner witnessing everything. "So I don't think there should be any doubts as to why I or any girl would want to go on a date with you."

"I am pretty good looking, aren't I?" He grinned at me. "Okay, let me get the drinks."

"Okay, thanks," I said, and I smiled to myself as I watched him walking toward the bar. Before I knew what was happening, Nolan was headed to our table with a scowl on his face. "Hey, Nolan."

"You're really just going to sit there smiling?" He looked annoyed.

"What?"

"He basically said he wanted you to lick him all over."

"What?" My voice was louder now. "What are you talking about?"

"When he was speaking Spanish, he said something like you're so sexy. I wish I could feel your lips on me."

"What? No, he didn't."

"Trust me, he did."

"Why didn't you say something before?"

"Because you were giving him an attitude, and I thought you were over him, but then you guys talked..." He rolled his eyes. "And now you're acting like everything is okay."

"Okay," I said, my voice short.

"I wanted to come over here and let you know he's still a pig." Nolan's handsome face looked aggravated. "Just because you think you're having some come to Jesus moment with him..."

"Come to Jesus moment?" I shook my head at him. "What?"

"I don't know. Maybe that was the wrong term to use. I just meant, just because you feel like you've bonded over the fact that you both have parents or backgrounds that are..." His voice trailed off and I gave him a look.

"That are what, Nolan?"

"You know." He shrugged.

"Nope." I narrowed my eyes at him. "What?"

"Sigh," he said out loud. "Why are you so difficult, Jules? Why can't you just trust me?"

"This is a first date, Nolan. I'm not about to marry the guy." I rolled my eyes. "And just because we both have diverse backgrounds doesn't mean I'm going to drop my panties for him." I glared at him but to my surprise all he did was laugh. "What's so funny?"

"I just never expected to ever hear you say drop my panties." He winked at me. "But I wouldn't mind you doing that for me."

"Nolan! That is so inappropriate."

"Why?" He licked his lips slowly as he stared at me. His eyes devoured my face and then looked down at my chest. "It's the truth."

"It's inappropriate because I'm here on a date with someone else."

"Then hurry up and end the date."

"Why?"

"So we can do something."

"What?" My jaw dropped. Was Nolan asking me out? What was going on here? I'd never seen Nolan like this before. And he'd certainly never asked me to do anything as just the two of us. Never.

"Hey, everything going okay?" Jose walked back to the

table with the drinks with a huge smile. "I hope you're making me look good on camera, man."

"As if anything could make you look bad," I said to Jose. "Thanks for the drink." I took it from his hand and sipped. "Oh this is so good."

"You're welcome. Cheers." He held up his beer mug to me.

"Cheers," I said and then looked over at Nolan who had taken to scowling again. "Anything else?"

"No," he said tightly. "Nothing else, *mi corazon*."

"Sorry what?" I asked him, not understanding what he'd just said.

"Nothing." He walked away and headed back to where his camera sat upon the tripod.

"That camera guy," Jose said looking at me and then at Nolan. "Do you know him or something?"

"I would hope so, he is my cameraman." I laughed.

"But do you know him as more than a cameraman?"

"Well, he's my best friend's brother."

"Oh, Beach Canyon." He laughed as he shook his head. "I forgot how small this town was. I guess you're a local."

"Yeah, born and bred here."

"Cool. It's a nice town, though to be honest, it's a bit small for me."

"Oh?"

"Yeah." He nodded. "I moved here because it was close to the beach and affordable, but there's like nothing going on."

"So you're going to move then?" I asked curiously. Not that I really cared about his answer. My mind was still on Nolan and his asking me to do something. What had he wanted to do with me?

"I suppose if I say yes, you're not going to sleep with me tonight."

"I was never going to sleep with you tonight."

"Oh yeah, I guess that wouldn't look good for your article."

"It has nothing to do with the article. I'm not interested in sleeping with you."

"I'm not cute enough?" He gave me an impish smile and I shook my head.

"Yeah, you're definitely not cute enough."

"Ouch, my heart has been broken," he said and I noticed he was looking back at the bar.

"Is everything okay?" I asked.

"Well, yeah, but, look, Sandy, the bartender, has made it clear that she's willing to have some fun tonight and well, you know..." He shrugged as he took another chug of his beer.

"No, what?"

"You're a nice girl and all, Jules, but we haven't really hit it off and I don't think we're looking for the same thing."

"Oh, okay." I felt humiliated. I couldn't believe that this shit was being documented.

"I mean, I think it was pretty clear from my profile that I wanted to bump and grind and well, you seem to want to go on some philosophical debate on something."

"WHAT?" My jaw dropped. "What are you talking about?"

"Look, girl, I'm not here for any deep talks, I'm here to salsa, if you know what I mean?" He raised his eyebrows and did a little dance and I just stared at him speechless. I could see Nolan standing behind his camera laughing and I couldn't believe it.

"You know what, just go." I placed my drink on the table. "This date is over."

"That's what I've been saying, *chica*." He nodded. "My only hope is I look good on the camera."

"Whatever." I jumped up and headed over to Nolan. "Let's go."

"What happened?" he asked, pretending to look confused.

"Not now, Nolan. Let's go."

"Where are we going?"

"I don't know." I shrugged. "Take me somewhere I can get drunk," I said and with that Nolan packed up his equipment quickly and we headed out of the bar. I looked back as we exited and I could see Jose flirting with Sandy and laughing at something she was saying.

"Do you want to talk about it?" Nolan said as we got into his car.

"Do I look like I want to talk about it?" I said shaking my head. "I'm confused as heck."

"He wasn't the guy for you."

"I know that. I'm just confused as to what happened. How am I supposed to write about dating when I don't even understand the date myself?"

"He was a douchebag, Jules."

"Sigh," I said and then actually let out a long deep sigh and buried my face in my hands. "This sucks. In fact, this actually sucks more than I thought it was going to suck when Malcolm pitched this idea to me."

"You looked good on camera, does that help?" Nolan offered with a small smile and I laughed slightly.

"A little bit." I grinned. "Ugh, why do men have to be so predictable?"

"Oh?"

"You guys only think with your small head."

"Small head?" he asked as he started the engine.

"You know what I mean?"

"Do I?" He chuckled, and I hit him in the shoulder. "Explain it to me."

"No, Nolan, I won't be explaining anything to you," I said. "Where are we going?"

"I'm going to stop by Al's liquor to get you some ciders and me some beers, then I'm going to drive to my place."

"Nolan!" I looked at him shocked. Was he suggesting what I thought he was suggesting?

"To park, Jules." He grinned. "I don't want to drink and drive. I was thinking I could park and then we could walk down to the beach and start a fire in one of the fire pits."

"Ooh that would be cool."

"You have blankets?"

"Yes, Jules."

"From other dates you've taken there or...." My voice trailed off as I realized the words I'd used. I hoped he didn't notice that I'd said from other dates, as if I was calling this a date.

"No, Jules. Actually, I don't take dates down to the beach at night," he said with a small smile. "Don't want to give anyone the wrong idea."

"The wrong idea?"

"Taking a date to the beach at night is quite intimate," he said.

"Really?" I scoffed. "I don't think it's that intimate." I made a face, but then I remembered something. "Oh, well, maybe to you but that's only because your dad proposed to your mom there one night. To most people, it's not that intimate of a date." I thought of his parents and the epic proposal his dad had done for his mom. He had taken her out to watch the stars and had already set up three hundred and sixty-five rose petals on the sand, one for each day he'd known her. He hadn't thought it through properly and the cleanup afterward had taken him a couple of hours. That night had been the night of a meteorite shower and as they'd watched the sky, he'd declared that his undying love was bigger than the universe and oceans combined and would she marry him. Obviously, Mrs. Montgomery had said yes and from what I could see they were still madly in love. I had no idea why Nolan was so opposed to marriage and serious relationships, but I didn't think we were close enough for me to ask him that.

"It's a special place." He shrugged. "Not a place to take anyone I've dated thus far."

"Okay," I said, but I wanted to ask him why he was taking me, but I suppose I was a longtime family friend, so I didn't really count. Yes, he had kissed me, but it had all been in good fun. He'd turned me down so many times before, he'd made it quite obvious that he wasn't interested in anything more with me.

12

"Are you cold?" Nolan asked me as we sat and watched the ocean from his blanket. "I can give you my sweater if you want."

"No, I'm okay, thanks." I shook my head and gave him a small smile before taking a sip of my cider. "It's beautiful out here at night. I always forget that. I should come out here more often."

"This is one of the main perks of living in Canyon Beach." Nolan nodded toward the ocean and jumped up suddenly. "Take your shoes off and come with me." He held his hand down to pull me up and I smiled at him quizzically as I stood.

"Where are we going?" I slipped my sandals off and put my bottle down on the blanket.

"For a walk," he said and tugged on my hand. "Let's go."

"You're so demanding, aren't you?"

"Never," he said with a laugh as we set off walking. "So are you upset?" He looked at my face as we walked along the side toward the water.

"Upset?" I stared at him, feeling confused. "Upset about what?"

"Jose," he said looking away from me. He bent down and picked up some shells from the sand and showed them to me. They looked almost translucent in the moonlight and I stared at them transfixed by their beauty.

"No, not at all," I said with a quick laugh. "I was a little confused, yes, and slightly offended, but upset? No, not at all."

"You didn't wish that he'd asked you on a second date?"

"No." I shook my head. "I wouldn't have said yes if he had asked."

"Then why did you agree to go on a date with him?"

"Why?" I thought about it for a moment. "He looked cute and well, I had a vision of him making me empanadas."

"Enchiladas?" he asked.

"No empanadas."

"What?" It was his turn to be confused, and I started laughing at the absurdity of the entire situation. As I laughed, Nolan's expression changed from confused to bemused and he just stared at me with that sweet sexy look on his face that always made me melt. It reminded me of the times he'd been there to cheer me on or tease me as a teenager or in college. He'd always looked at me as if he wasn't quite sure what to make of me.

"It's stupidness, really." I sighed as I finally stopped laughing. "I knew the date wasn't going to be great from the messages, but I still felt he was the best of the bunch." I perked up as I just remembered that I'd seen that Lucas had sent me a message on the dating app right before I'd met up with Jose. I went to reach for my phone but I didn't want Nolan to tease me.

"What's got you so happy all of a sudden?" Nolan looked at me suspiciously. "Oh wait, don't tell me you got another letter from Fitz?"

"Actually, yes, I did," I said with a small smile. "And he also sent me a message on a dating app."

"He what?" Nolan's jaw dropped. "How did he do that?"

"He joined the app and messaged me, silly." I laughed and pulled my phone out. "See." I brought up the app and showed him Lucas's profile.

"That's Lucas Sacramento."

"Yeah, I know that."

"He told you he's Fitz?"

"No, not yet," I admitted. "But it has to be him." Nolan gazed at me for a few seconds and he seemed to be thinking about something.

"So, have you written him back yet?"

"No, I'm going to message him later."

"I meant Fitz," Nolan said stiffly. "Have you written him a letter?"

"No, I'll do that tomorrow or something." I shrugged. "Why?"

"No reason." He took out a pack of gum and offered me a piece. I shook my head no and he continued. "Do you know what you're going to say in your article?"

"Yeah, maybe to not be superficial and to not just swipe for good looks." I nodded as I realized the idea that had just popped to my mind made actual sense. "I mean let's be real, everyone knows guys just want to swipe on hot women, but a lot of times women give good-looking guys a pass in the bad personality department, just because they're cute. It's just not a good way to date. And well...." My words drifted off as I didn't really want to tell him the rest of my thoughts.

"Well, what?" he asked me, his eyes gazing into mine as he took a step closer to me.

"Well, just because a guy is good-looking doesn't mean he's good in bed." I reddened as his gaze became more interested.

"Is that right?" He cocked his head to the side. "This is something you know to be true?"

"This is something I know to be true," I said with a nod, though it wasn't something I knew to be true from experience, rather from talking to friends about it.

"So, you've been with a lot of good-looking men then?" He grabbed my hands and pulled me to him. He looked down into my eyes and I could feel the warmth of his body seeping into mine. My thighs felt like they were on fire when his leg casually bumped into mine.

"Well, not exactly." I could barely get the words out. I was so breathless and captivated by his smile.

"Do you think I'm good-looking?"

"You're okay," I said quickly looking him over dismissively. No way was I going to tell him how drop-dead gorgeous I thought he was. Or how being so close to him made my entire insides want to tremble and melt against him.

"Just okay?" he said with a chuckle as his lips came down on mine.

"Just okay." I nodded slowly, my lips pressed against his lightly. My heart was racing, and I wanted to just pull him into me even harder and kiss him. Before I knew what I was doing, my arms were around his neck and I was kissing him hard. His lips pressed against mine and he kissed me back just as hard, his hands fell to my ass and I could taste the IPA he'd just been drinking on his lips.

"You taste like apples," he whispered against my lips as he tugged on my lower lip with his teeth. He sucked on my lip and I melted against him. His hands slid up my back to the nape of my neck and his fingers played with my hair. I could feel his hardness next to my belly as he pushed into me and my legs trembled slightly at the feel of him. His chest was warm to the touch as I reached my fingers up under his shirt. I ran my fingers across his abs and the tightness of his muscles always amazed me. I wondered how often he worked out. Not that I was going to ask. I didn't want him to know how perfect I thought his body was. His lips moved from mine and started to kiss down my neck and then to the spot just below my ear.

"I want you." He groaned as he blew into my ear, the feel of his breath tickling me and I gasped. "I want to taste you."

"What?" My fingers played with his hair and I felt my breasts crushed against his muscular chest.

"I want to taste all of you. I want to see if your wet pussy tastes like apples as well."

I gasped loudly then and my eyes widened as he stared at me.

"Does that shock you?" he asked as his hand slid up under my skirt and along my thighs. He reached up to the hem of my panties and he grinned as he slipped my panties to the side and touched me gently with his fingers. "I knew you were wet."

"Nolan." I groaned. "What are you doing?"

"What do you want me to be doing?"

"I don't know."

"You don't know?" he asked a sly smile on his face as he moved my panties away from me. "You really don't know?"

"Nolan," I said, not knowing what he was really asking of me. "I..." My voice trailed off as he kissed me again and this time there was no hesitancy on his part. He kissed me as if he'd been waiting all his life to have his lips taste mine. He kissed me as if he couldn't get enough of me and I kissed him back as well. All of our chemistry and headbutting was finally coming to a head and it was explosive.

"Let's go back to the blanket." He growled as he picked me up and carried me back down the beach.

"I thought we were going for a walk." I squealed.

"You still want to walk?" He looked shocked.

"I wouldn't mind feeling the waves on my feet." I smiled shyly. "I love the ocean."

"You love the ocean, huh?" He grinned and before I knew what was happening he was running back toward the water and laughing.

"Nolan, what are you doing?" I squirmed against him as I realized he was headed into the water. "Nolan," I screamed out as he let me down gently and I felt the cold swoosh of water covering my legs. He grinned at me and then bent down and pushed a small wave of water on me and splashed me.

"Here's the water you wanted." He laughed as I reached down and started swatting the cold water onto him. We splashed each other back and forth for a good couple of minutes and then he pulled me against him and started kissing me passionately. I melted against him and ran my hands down his back. He pulled away from me and grabbed my hand and we walked back to the blanket.

"I guess you're not thinking about Lucas right now," he said as we lay down on the blanket and his hand fondled my breast. His eyes were gleaming and he had a secretive smile on his face.

"I need to go home." I jumped up suddenly, even though my body missed the touch of him. "I'm cold and wet and I need to shower and change."

He looked at me for a few seconds as if he wanted to change my mind, but he just nodded and gathered up his stuff.

"Okay then, I'll take you home." And with that, our moment was done.

❧ 13 ❧

"Heathcliff, I'm home," I sang out as I entered my front door after waving goodbye to Nolan. The drive home held felt awkward, and I really hadn't known what to say. My brain felt all sorts of discombobulated as I settled into the couch and played with Heathcliff's ears. Why was this all so bloody complicated? My life had gone from zero to two hundred in a mere couple of weeks and I wasn't sure I could handle all the adventure. Heathcliff whined at my feet as I got ready to turn the TV on. "You want a treat?" I asked him and he whined again. I sighed as I realized that I needed to take him on a walk, a long walk. I'd let him out in the garden to do his business, but he wanted to actually run. "Okay, boy." I yawned as I got up and headed toward the coat rack where I kept his leash. "C'mon, let's go for a walk. Lucas can wait," I said as if Heathcliff cared at all. Heathcliff ran toward me, tongue hanging out and tail wagging and I knew that he was extremely happy at the fact he was going for a late night walk. "Ugh, you know that this means I'm going to have a very late night. I have to respond to Lucas and I have to write my article for tomorrow. Malcolm has texted me three times tonight to see how the date went and I can't just write, 'it was a hot mess, the end,' or I will lose my job." I moaned as Heathcliff sniffed along the street, not paying any attention to me. I walked him for another fifteen minutes before heading back home again.

He ran to the kitchen to drink some water while I settled back on the couch and picked up my phone. I was excited to read Lucas's message on the dating app. I decided that I would send him a letter and a response to his message and tell him some of the same things. That way he would definitely know that I knew it was him.

I clicked on his message and read eagerly, reading it out loud to savor it. "Sup, Jules, how's it going? Remember me from school? I look a bit different, but so do you. Who knew you'd get so hot? Wanna grab a drink and catch up some time. Maybe discuss some of the best books we've read recently? Lucas." My jaw dropped as I finished reading his message. "Oh my God, Heathcliff," I shouted to my dog because I had no one else to talk to. "Heathcliff, he just outted himself." I was so excited I could barely contain it. I pulled out his last letter again and looked at his message. In both pieces of correspondence, he had commented on the fact that he loved books. He'd basically just confirmed what I already knew. I thought it was so sweet that he was using my love of books to connect with me. I smiled to myself as I responded to his message on the dating site first.

Hey Lucas, of course, I remember you! I heard you just got back into town. It would be great to catch up and talk books! :) When were you thinking of getting together? Jules

I pressed send and then I got ready to write him a letter, but I realized that it was close to midnight and I still hadn't done any swiping or messaging and I hadn't written my first article, plus there was a slight melancholy in my soul as I thought of Nolan and our time together. I lightly touched my lips as I thought about the press of his lips against mine. The moment had felt magical and meant to be, but I knew that to Nolan, I was nothing but a fling and someone to mess around with. He had turned me down too many times, and I wasn't going to let him hurt me again.

I closed my eyes and tried to stop the memory of my biggest disappointment from playing in my head, but I couldn't. It had been the weekend that Nolan and Jackson had visited me in college. I'd been a senior and about to graduate, excited about the fact that I'd gotten a reporting job at the *Canyon Beach Chronicle*. My boyfriend Mark and I had just broken up because, frankly, the relationship had sucked. He'd been awful in bed and I had never orgasmed from the five-minute sex we'd had. He'd always seemed more obsessed with trying to slip it in the backdoor than trying to pleasure me and most of our time in bed was me telling him no to anal and then him coming quickly on my stomach.

Only Stella and Betsy knew how bad he'd been in bed and I'd sworn them to secrecy. When we'd broken up, I hadn't been that devastated, but when Nolan had said he was coming to visit, I'd pretended to be upset over my breakup with Mark so that I could save face. I didn't want Nolan thinking that I'd harbored a crush on him since high school. That first night Nolan had been so sweet to me and taken me to dinner. He had been older and more mature, having been out of college for a few years and we'd had a really fun night. And then we'd gone back to my room to watch a movie. He'd kissed me so tenderly and I'd kissed him back passionately. He'd removed my clothes and taken me with his tongue and I'd orgasmed into his mouth, my whole body trembling with pleasure and then because I'd been so overwhelmed and happy, I'd started crying. I hadn't been crying out of pain though, I'd been crying from pleasure. However, Nolan had frozen and asked me what was wrong and I'd told him that I was still upset over my breakup with Mark. I hadn't wanted him to know that I thought I was in love with him. I mean, how crazy would that have been? And before I knew what was happening, Nolan was pulling my clothes back on me and jumping up and telling me he had to leave. He'd told me that I wasn't in the right emotional state to just hook up and that that was all that he'd wanted and he'd left. I cried more tears than I'd ever cried for Mark. Just thinking about that night in combination with my first kiss and asking him to sleep with me was enough to make me weary about being with Nolan in any way. He had a track record of breaking my heart and just walking away. I had been right to end things before they went further this evening. Nolan Montgomery could not be trusted with my heart and I wasn't going to go down that road with him again.

'

❧ 14 ❧

"This article is wonderful, Jules. Just wonderful." Malcolm looked up from his screen and beamed. "We're going to have it go live as soon as Nolan sends us the edited video." He nodded happily to himself. "This should get us a lot of hits."

"I hope so."

"I've already had some calls from other businesses in town that want to sponsor some of the dates and buy ads."

"Wow, really?" I was slightly confused. "But how come? The first article isn't even up yet. How do they even know about it?" But as I spoke the words, I realized that I already knew the answer. This was Canyon Beach, everyone knew everyone's business, sometimes even before they knew it themselves. "Actually, no need to answer. I already know."

"So when's the next date?"

"Going to work on that now, hopefully in a couple of days," I said with a small smile, not wanting to tell him anything about Lucas.

"And how are you and Nolan working together?"

"Yeah, it's fine." I shrugged, ignoring the image of his

body against mine and the way his fingers had touched me the night before.

"Good, good," he said with a small smile. "Okay, well, get to work. I'm excited for your next article."

"Thanks, Malcolm," I said as I stood up and walked back to my desk. I checked my phone to see if there were any new messages from Lucas but there weren't. He really wasn't very fast to respond and I was starting to find it all a bit annoying. I picked up the letter I'd written before bed and decided to drop it off at the post office and then grab a cupcake and coffee from Betsy's shop.

Dearest Fitz,

I've heard about that book and will definitely check it out. I just recently read Truly Devious by Maureen Johnson and it was amazing. It is a YA thriller/murder mystery, but so much more than that. Have you been dating much since you've been back in town? It would be great to catch up and talk books! Hope to hear back from you soon.

Jules

If he didn't get the hint from this letter, he was never going to get the hint. I hurried to the post office and dropped my letter in the post box. As I was walking out, I saw Nolan at the counter talking to someone. I was about to leave when he looked up and noticed me.

"Hey Jules," he said as he hurried over to me. "How's it going?" His eyes searched mine as he gave me a wide smile and I pretended that my heart hadn't just jumped out of my body when I'd seen him.

"I'm good. Just dropping off a letter for Lucas."

"You mean Fitz?" he asked with a slight look.

"Yeah, Fitz." I shrugged. "What about you? You're in the post office a lot these days?"

"Oh?"

"Your 'friend' Ellen said you guys were coming to the post office the other day as well."

"Oh yes, she did." He grinned. "Good memory."

"Hmm." I frowned. "Are you still seeing her?"

"I was never seeing her, Jules." He winked at me and I could feel myself growing angry.

"Oh, so just having sex?" I was annoyed at the fact that he seemed to just be able to go from woman to woman. "What are you, a sex machine?"

"No." He laughed and grabbed my hands. "Ellen is a friend. She's been coming over to get help with her new camera. She wants to become a wedding photographer."

"Yeah right." I tried not to roll her eyes. The only wedding she wanted to photograph was the one between her and Nolan. Though, of course, I didn't say that.

"Are you jealous?" he asked as his fingers touched the side of my face and his eyes sparkled as if he were laughing at me.

"Jealous of what? I could have had sex with you, as well, if I wanted to." I pushed him away from me, starting to feel flushed. His lips turned up and he moved closer to me.

"I think you did want to," he whispered into my ear and I could feel his breath on my skin. I trembled slightly as I stared into his beautiful green eyes.

"What do you want from me, Nolan?" I said pushing against his chest, swallowing hard as he kissed me lightly on the lips. "What are you doing?"

"What do you think I'm doing?" he said as he kissed me again.

"You can't just keep kissing me."

"Don't tell me you're still not over Mark."

"Who?" I blinked at him in confusion.

"The ex you were crying over in college?" His eyes studied my face. "That weekend I came up. The weekend I gave you that gift."

"Oh yeah, Mark." I laughed then. "I actually haven't thought about him in years. So yes, I'm over him."

"Good, good." He grinned. "So you never told me what you thought about my gift by the way, did you like it?"

"Gift?" I blinked again. "Oh yeah, I never opened that. I put it in my suitcase and forgot about it." I made a guilty face. "Sorry." I laughed as he frowned. "It's not a big deal, right? It wasn't diamonds or something."

"No diamonds," he said and then a light suddenly appeared in his eyes. "Aww, that's why," he said as if to himself.

"That's why, what?" I asked him, confused. I wanted to reach up and touch his hair that had fallen across his forehead, but I knew that it would give him the wrong signal.

"A lady's imagination is very rapid; it jumps from admiration to love, from love to matrimony, in a moment," he said in an English accent and I just stared at him in absolute confusion.

"What?"

"It's from *Pride and Prejudice*," he said gazing into my eyes intently. "It's one of Mr. Darcy's lines."

"Oh, okay, I must have forgotten," I said nonchalantly. "I haven't read that book in years."

"You used to love Jane Austen though," he said with a small frown. "I thought she was your favorite author."

"I mean, yeah, I went through a phase where I loved her, but that was years ago." I laughed. "Don't get me wrong, she's an amazing author, but I didn't memorize all of her books or anything."

"I guess you had enough time remembering Juliet's lines." He chuckled.

"Hey, I was awesome as Juliet." I grinned at him. "I was a natural."

"A natural kisser," he said and I made a face at him.

"Do not remind me of that night," I said and shuddered. "That was so embarrassing."

"Actually, I thought it was quite cute. In fact..." He started, but I stopped paying attention to him because about five yards away stood Lucas Sacramento and he was headed into the post office. "Earth to Jules?" he said and then turned around to see what I was looking at. "Who's that?"

"That's Lucas, aka Fitz," I mumbled. "Oh my gosh," I said and like magic, Lucas turned around and spotted me.

"Julia Montgomery?" he said a wide smile spreading across his face as he approached me with outstretched arms.

"Lucas Sacramento?" I asked him, trying to ignore the fact that he had some envelopes in his hand. Was he sending me another letter? He swept me into a big hug and gave me a big kiss on the cheek. I could see Nolan standing there with a scowl on his face, but I ignored him.

"How have you been?" Lucas grinned at me. "I was just about to send you a message for a date."

"Oh yeah?" I smiled up at him. His big blue eyes were bluer than I remembered them being and he had filled out nicely. "A message or a letter?" I said jokingly looking at the letters in his hand.

"A message," he said smoothly. "I can't believe we matched on the dating app. How fortuitous."

"Yes, it's not like we would have spoken any other way." I laughed at my joke. "Though I guess written words aren't actually spoken."

"Uh, yeah," he said as he looked my body over in a way that let me know that he very much liked what he was seeing. It should have made me feel good inside, but his look repulsed me slightly. He was a bit too lecherous in his glance; I mean he hadn't seen me in years. "So, I guess I don't need to message anymore. What about tomorrow night?"

"Tomorrow?" I said, seeing that Nolan's face was not happy at all. What was his problem?

"I can't do tomorrow." Nolan almost barked. "That won't work."

"Huh?" Lucas turned toward him, his face confused. "Who are... wait, is that you, Nolan? Nolan Montgomery?"

"Yes." Nolan looked surprised that Lucas knew who he was. "I didn't realize you knew me."

"Ha, everyone in our literature class knew you. Jules talked about you all the time." Lucas looked toward me, his expression slightly unfocused. "Didn't you have a huge crush on him in high school?" He nodded. "Yeah, you did. Wait are you guys dating?"

"No," I screeched out, my face red. "No, no, and no." And then I turned to Nolan. "This is a real date, not a date for the paper, you don't need to be there."

"I don't think that's allowed." He gave me a death glare, and I wondered what his problem was.

"Sorry, what are you two talking about? Why is Nolan going on your dates?"

"It's a long story," I said. "I'll tell you about it tomorrow night."

"Aww, okay." Lucas grinned, and I watched as he brushed his hair back from his face. "Sounds good. So I, better just pop into the post office but I'll see you tomorrow?"

"Sounds good." I nodded.

"I'll message you," he said with a smile and I laughed.

"Better message on the app and not by mail." I grinned at him, but he just gave me a blank stare.

"Uh, yeah. Bye sweetness," he said and before I knew it he was giving me a firm kiss on the lips before he headed off. "And there will be more of that waiting for you tomorrow." He winked and walked away with me standing there with my jaw open.

"You're really going to go out with that douche?" Nolan stared at me with narrowed eyes. "Really, Jules?"

"I mean, he sent me really sweet letters. He's just shy," I mumbled, but even as I said the words, they didn't ring true. Would a shy guy really have kissed me like that?

"Yeah, he's shy. Keep telling yourself that. You'll be saying he tripped and his dick just slipped in as well."

"Nolan!" I exclaimed, shocked at his words. "What's your problem?"

"I can't believe you think he's Fitz." He shook his head. "You're totally just in your head, aren't you?"

"What the hell is that supposed to mean?"

"It means that you only see what you want to see."

"Okay, Nolan, whatever." I sighed. "I'm off to Betsy's to grab a coffee and cupcake so I have to go."

"You know she's not there, right?"

"Huh?" I blinked. "What do you mean? Where is she?"

"She's at the police station," he said a smug look on his face. "Delivering cupcakes to Jeff and the guys."

"She what?" My jaw dropped. "Is she dating Jeff?"

"What?" It was his turn to look shocked. "Of course not. She just likes to donate cupcakes to the police force."

"Uh-huh." I shook my head. "And I'm the one that sees what I want to see." I grabbed my phone and saw that I had some messages from some new guys on my dating apps. "Looks like work calls, I've just received some messages from some new guys."

"Why don't you let me help you choose your next date?" he asked with a grin. "I feel like you need some help."

"Excuse me?"

"Well, Jose wasn't a great match and Lucas doesn't seem much better."

"Lucas isn't a work date," I protested but he held his hand up.

"Come on, let's go to Betsy's. Grandma Elsie is there today and she'll hook us up." He grinned as my expression changed. He knew how much I loved Grandma Elsie and he also knew that she hooked me up with a lot more cupcakes than Betsy did.

"Fine," I said with a sigh. "Let's go."

"OH MY DEARS, IS TODAY MY LUCKY DAY OR WHAT?" Grandma Elsie beamed as we walked into the coffee shop. "My favorite grandson and my granddaughter's favorite friend."

"I'm your only grandson, Nana." Nolan laughed as he hugged her. "And Jules is Betsy's oldest friend."

"Hi, Grandma Elsie." I gave her a hug. "Nolan and I just came to do some work."

"Ooh yes, for your dating articles, right? You guys must be working very hard together."

"Uh yeah," I said as she continued to beam at me.

"I did tell your parents and Malcolm that I thought this would be a great idea."

"It was your idea?" I asked, surprised as she handed me over a plate of cupcakes. "What? Why?"

"Well, I did remember how well you and Nolan worked together in high school," she continued as she started pouring two cups of coffee.

"We did?"

"When he helped you with your play dear..." She smiled at me as she handed me the cup. "The milk's over there. Go easy on the sugar."

"Thank you." I blushed as she mentioned the play. "Oh yeah."

"Though I don't suppose you need much help with kissing anymore," she said and my face went redder.

"Grandma Elsie, stop." Nolan laughed as he took his cup of coffee from her. "You're making Jules blush."

"I'm not blushing," I said and took a quick sip of coffee. "Hmm delicious."

"We got some new free trade beans from Kenya." Grandma Elsie nodded. "They are very good."

"This coffee tastes almost as good as your lips," Nolan whispered to me as he sat down across from me and I gave him a sharp look. "What?" He smiled innocently as I swatted his hand.

"Nothing." I glared at him.

"Oh, you two," Grandma Elsie laughed. "Still acting like you did when you were youngsters."

"No," I protested, but then laughed as I realized she was right. "I guess we bring that out in each other."

"I guess so." She smiled sweetly. "I always did wonder why the two of you never dated; especially after Nolan gave you that *Pride and Prejudice* first edition."

"Huh?" I blinked, confused. "What first edition?"

"She never opened it, Nana." Nolan shook his head at her. "She didn't even know I gave it to her."

"Oh, but didn't she see what you wrote in it?"

"Nope." He shook his head and gave me a wry smile. "Anyway, we have work to do." He smiled at her. "So we need to concentrate."

"I get the hint." Her voice tinkled, and she stared at us for a few seconds before walking away. "They'll figure it out," she said under her breath and even though I didn't know what she was talking about, I didn't bother asking her to explain.

"So we have John, Oliver, and Barry lined up as good potential dates," Nolan said after we'd gone through all my messages. "They seem interesting and will make for good articles."

"Barry has a foot fetish," I said, shaking my head. "And John says that he likes to wear women's panties." I glared at Nolan as he burst out laughing. "These guys are not good potential dates."

"They are good potential stories, plus, I thought you were all about Lucas?" he said with narrowed eyes.

"I'm not all about Lucas," I protested, and then sighed. "I don't know, I want to give him a chance. His letters really made me feel good in high school and college and well, he just dropped off of the face of the earth. And I was never able to tell him."

"Oh why?"

"He never left a return address before. And he never revealed himself. I always wanted to know who he was. Always wanted to meet him."

"And you always hoped it was him?" he asked me with his head cocked to the side.

"Well, no..." My voice trailed off. How could I tell Nolan that I'd always hoped it was him that had been sending the letters? That I'd dreamed about him revealing himself to me and sweeping me off of my feet. Obviously, that hadn't happened and I didn't want him to feel awkward. "So, tell me about you, why do you have such an aversion to long-term relationships?"

"Who said I had an aversion?" His smile was wide as he sat back.

"Well, you've never been in one and you're always telling me all you do is hookups. Like in college..." My voice trailed off again.

"Oh that," he said with a frown. "That wasn't exactly true."

"Oh?"

"I didn't just want a hookup, but I didn't want to take advantage of you."

"Take advantage of me?"

"You were crying over Mark." He sighed. "What sort of man would I be to sleep with a woman still in tears over her ex. I wasn't going to be that guy, no matter how much I wanted you."

"Oh." I bit my lower lip and thought hard. Should I tell him that I hadn't been crying because of Mark? Should I tell him that I'd been crying out of happiness and that my body had been delirious with the pleasure that he'd given me? No, I couldn't tell him that. It was embarrassing to have him know that his tongue had given me more pleasure than my ex's cock.

"Yeah, so that was why." He leaned forward now. "I'd quite like a relationship with the right girl."

"Oh?" I was surprised and my heart started racing. "Really?"

"Really." He grinned. "But until I meet her, I'm ready to just have some fun."

"Oh, I see." My heart dropped then. He just wanted to have fun with me. "Well, I better go now, I'm sure Malcolm is wondering where I am."

"Oh, okay." Nolan paused for a few seconds as if he wanted to say something else. "I sent him the video so I guess your first article will be going live soon."

"Yes, it will." I groaned. "Only twenty-nine more dates to go," I said and jumped up. "Well, I'll be seeing you. Bye, Nolan, bye, Grandma Elsie."

❧ 15 ❧

"**B**etsy Montgomery, you better call me back ASAP," I said to her answering machine as I arrived home after work. "A little birdy told me you were at the police station. What's going on?" I said before I hung up the phone and headed to my bedroom. "Hey, Heathcliff." I patted my dog as he looked up from my bed. "I'm looking for a gift that Nolan gave me," I said as I opened my closet. "Where had I put that package?" I rifled through my things and when I came up empty, I sat on the bed and tried to think. As I was sitting my phone started ringing, and I grabbed it, surprised to see Nolan's number and not Betsy's.

"Oh hey," I said as I answered the phone. "What's up?"

"Were you expecting someone else?"

"Yes, actually," I said and he laughed. I didn't bother telling him that I was waiting on a call back from Betsy. Let him think I had lots of guys after me.

"What are you doing tonight?"

"Tonight?"

"Yes, tonight."

"Nothing, why?"

"I was thinking we could play a board game or something," he said smoothly. "And you could bring me a bottle of wine this time."

"You want me to play a board game with you?" I was shocked. "Why?"

"Because I think it will be fun. Or do you not agree?"

"Can I not agree?"

"Come over at seven. I'll order a pizza."

"Yes, boss," I said and with that, he laughed and hung up. "Well, that was Nolan," I said to Heathcliff who had already gone back to dozing against my pillow. "He wants me to come over to hang out. It's totally not a big deal," I said. "I bet he just wants sex. Well, little does he know, I'm not about to just hook up with him," I said out loud again and in my mind I really meant it. That didn't stop me from running to the shower to wash my hair and shave though. And when I say shave I meant everywhere (just in case, of course).

"I CANNOT BELIEVE THAT YOU BEAT ME." NOLAN GRABBED his can of beer and chugged it down. "Again." He groaned as I did a little victory dance.

"Well, I am the Queen of Monopoly," I said laughing, feeling slightly tipsy from the lemon drop cocktails he had made me. "And Uno."

"You've gone from the Queen of First Dates to the Queen of Uno," he said and stood up and moved closer to me. "What shall we do now?" he said as he stopped in front of me.

"I don't know," I whispered as I stared up at him, my heart racing as I gazed into his warm eyes. He gave me a huge smile and then grabbed me around the waist and pulled me toward him.

"Well, it's a good thing I do then," he said as his lips crushed down on mine. It only took three seconds for me to kiss him back passionately and my arms went around his neck and my fingers went into his hair. His hands reached under my top and his fingers lightly traced up my back before he pulled my top off. My bra soon followed and his lips were on my nipple, sucking and tugging gently. I moaned out loud and he looked up at me and grinned. I took the opportunity to pull his shirt off and before I knew it he was unbuckling my jeans and pulling them off, so that I was standing there in just a black thong. He stepped back and stared at my body for a few seconds and said, "Beautiful" under his breath before I reached over and unbuckled his belt. I pulled his jeans down and it was my turn to stare at him. He was wearing a pair of black briefs that clung to him and I could see his cock hard and protruding. I touched it lightly and then ran my fingers into the top of his boxer shorts. His breath caught, and he growled as he waited to see what I was going to do next. I didn't wait to see what he was going to do next and reached into his briefs and touched his bare cock with my fingers. It seemed to grow at my touch and my fingers stroked down the length of him to his tip. He growled again and pressed his lips against mine, his tongue invading my mouth roughly as my breasts crushed against his chest. His hands flew to my ass and his fingers slipped between my legs pressing up against my wetness and he rubbed gently. I could feel my legs buckling at his touch and he pulled me closer to him.

"Come." He grunted and he pulled me into his bedroom. He pushed me down on the bed and pulled his briefs down. I swallowed as his huge cock sprung forward and my breath caught as he leaned forward and started pulling my thong down with his teeth. "I'm still hungry after that pizza," he said as he kissed back up my thigh and I screamed slightly as I felt his lips closing in on my clit and sucking. My body bucked as his tongue entered me swiftly, moving in and out as confidently as any cock could. My fingers gripped his sheets as my eyes closed succumbing to the need to just focus on the pleasure coursing through my body. I could feel my orgasm building quickly. It had been so long since I'd been with a man and never had I been with one as skilled as Nolan. He paused for a second and before I knew what I was doing, I was gripping his head and pushing him back down. I needed to feel him against me, needed this release. He chuckled slightly as his tongue entered me again and I could feel his fingers playing with my nipples. My first orgasm came quickly after that and he licked my juices up as I came.

"You taste so sweet." He grunted as he sat up. He lifted me up and placed me on all fours. "Now it's my turn." He reached over to his nightstand, grabbed a condom wrapper, ripped it open, and slid it on his hardness, all within five seconds. He positioned himself behind me and I could feel the tip of his cock at my opening, teasing my clit and making me wet again. He grabbed my hair and pulled my head back as he slid into me. I cried out as his cock filled me. "Oh my," I cried out as he filled me, deep and hard, moving swiftly in and out of me so that I could feel every inch of him. How I compared his tongue to his cock, I had no idea. His tongue had felt magical but his cock felt surreal. His cock was taking me to places I had never been before. He slowed down his pace a bit and I felt his hands squeezing my breasts into his palms as he slid in and out of me, allowing me to feel and savor every single inch of him.

"Your pussy feels so good." He grunted in my ear and his right hand slid down my belly between my legs and rubbed my clit as he increased his speed again. I fell slightly forward as he thrust into me over and over again and my body shuddered and collapsed as I orgasmed once again. I felt Nolan's body stiffen behind me about a minute after I came and he held me tight as his cock lay inside of me for a few minutes before he pulled out and took the condom off. We lay back on the bed together and just stared at each other.

"Well, that was good," he said with a small smile as he kissed me on the lips and I just stared back at him feeling dazed and confused. He pulled me into his arms and we crawled under the sheets. "Was it good for you?"

"You know it was good for me," I said as I stroked his chest. "It was pretty amazing," I admitted as he started playing with my breasts again. "Aren't you tired?" I giggled as his finger slid between my legs again and I could feel his hardness growing on my hip.

"Nope," he said as he nibbled on my shoulder. "I'm ready to go again if you are, Elizabeth."

"Huh?" I blinked at him. "I'm Jules."

"I know." He laughed and kissed my forehead. "Trust me, I know."

❧ 16 ❧

I could feel every muscle in my body was achy and tired as I walked to the bar to meet up with Lucas. I had told Nolan that I was still going on this date and he hadn't said anything. If he had asked me not to go, I wouldn't have gone. I knew that in my bones. Even if Lucas was Fitz and had loved me for years. I couldn't see myself with him now, no matter how handsome he was. It just didn't matter. He just wasn't Nolan, and I knew after having had sex with Nolan that it had always been him and would always be him.

Even if he didn't know what he wanted. Even if I wasn't the one for him. Maybe I could convince him and maybe one day he would fall for me. I sighed as I walked into the bar and saw Lucas sitting there waiting for me with a hopeful smile on his face. I felt absolutely nothing for him as I walked toward him and wished that I was still in Nolan's bed. Sex with him had been everything I'd imagined it would be and so much more. I already missed feeling his cock inside of me. We'd showered together before I'd gone to work this morning and he'd been so gentle with me. I couldn't believe that we'd waited this long to finally sleep together and it seemed to me that I had rocked his world as well.

"Jules, you made it." Lucas stood up and came over and planted a kiss on my lips. "So glad to see you."

"And you," I lied as I sat down. "How's it going?"

"You know..." He shrugged. "Want a drink?"

"Sure. I'll have a glass of red wine please, a pinot noir."

"All right, coming up," he said and then called the waitress over. "So my dumb bitch of an ex-wife contacted me today."

"Oh?" I was taken aback at his words and choice of conversation. Was this really how he was going to start the date?

"She wants more alimony, but that bitch isn't getting shit."

"Oh, I'm sorry," I said because I didn't know what else to say.

"She claims I gave her herpes." He took a swig of his beer and then just started chugging.

"Oh no, that's not good." I looked around the bar wondering if anyone could hear us.

"No, it's not." He shook his head. "But it's all good. Here we are back together. The two English nerds."

"Here we are," I said with a weak smile.

"I was surprised to see that you were into non-monogamous relationships as well." He grinned at me. "Surprised, but happy. I'd love to bang you and another chick at the same time."

"Um, sorry what?" I frowned, my heart racing. What the hell was he talking about?

"My profile. I was surprised you messaged me back after we connected, but figured well, you never know who the kinky ones are."

"Your profile?" I blinked at him.

"On the dating app." He laughed. "There are not many

women that agree to meet a guy who's into non-monogamy and looking for a threesome."

"Say what?" I said and I could feel myself sweating. I realized then that I'd never actually read Lucas's profile. I'd been so excited that he'd matched with me after getting the letters that I hadn't felt that I'd needed to. "Threesome?"

"You're down right?" He leaned forward eagerly. "I know we didn't clarify if you prefer another man or another woman. To be fair, I don't do other cocks, but I don't mind double-teaming if you're cool with some girl on girl as well."

"Oh my." My face reddened. "I think there's been a mistake…" I stammered. "Um, you never said anything like this in your letters."

"What letters?" He frowned and it was then that my phone started ringing. I grabbed it from my pocket and saw that it was Betsy. Perfect timing.

"Excuse me, I have to take this," I said quickly, jumping up. "Betsy, oh my God, you will not believe where I am and with who," I burst out before she could speak. "And where have you been, I've been texting and calling you," I said.

"Oh Jules," she said, her voice teary. "I've messed up big time. I need your help."

"What?" I said confused. "What happened?"

"I can't talk about it right now, but can I come over tomorrow?"

"Uh yeah. What's going on?"

"I messed up big time."

"What did you do?"

"So, you know Jeff and…" Her voice trailed off and she cleared her voice. "Coming, Grandma Elsie. Look, Jules, I will explain it all tomorrow, but it's a big mess and I need for you to keep a secret."

"Betsy, you've got me so confused," I whined. "Can't you tell me now?"

"No," she said quickly. "I love you. See you tomorrow." And with that, she hung up. I looked at the blank screen and blinked, trying to figure out what she'd been talking about. It had to do with Jeff, that much was evident. But what could she have done that could have been so bad? Did she sleep with him? I froze as the thought hit me. Did she sleep with him and not tell me? I immediately felt guilty because I wasn't sure how I was going to tell her I slept with Nolan. In fact, I didn't even know if I should. I mean, I didn't know if that was going anywhere and was it fair to say anything if it wasn't? I walked back to the table, and I saw Lucas was swiping on the app as he'd been waiting for me. I knew then and there I was over it and him. I didn't care if he was Fitz. Maybe he'd been a sweet and romantic guy in high school and college but he had clearly changed.

"Hey, emergency, I have to go," I said before he could say a word. I turned around quickly and hurried out of the bar and headed home. As I walked in the door, I saw a text message from Nolan and I smiled. *"Hey, can I come over after your date? I have a feeling that he won't compare to me."* His text read and I laughed. I quickly texted him, "*Sure, come over in an hour,*" before I could overthink it and change my mind. I wanted to see him again and if I was honest, I wanted to have sex with him again. I didn't care what this was right now. I could worry about all the small details later. I then walked into the garage and started going through all my old boxes trying to locate the present Nolan had given me that weekend. He had never mentioned it to me until recently but it seemed like it had been a big deal, if even Grandma Elsie had known about it. I was close to crying when I got through the last box and still couldn't find it, but then I remembered that I had a box of kitchen stuff in a cupboard that I'd never opened and hurried inside again. It was a long shot, but it was worth a chance. I ran into the kitchen and pulled the box out of the cupboard and almost screamed in happiness when I saw the small neatly wrapped packaging that held the gift Nolan had given me. The wrapping was faded now, but I didn't care as I ripped it open to see a vintage copy of *Pride and Prejudice* sitting in my hands. I smiled to myself as I looked over the book and held it to my heart. It had been such a thoughtful gift. I opened the book to read the first page, and that was when I noticed that there was an inscription inside of it.

To my Dearest Jules,

I have loved you since I can remember. And I can remember a long time. When I gave you your first kiss as Juliet, I thought my heart would explode but I knew that it would be selfish of me to try and date you then. Plus, you were too young. So I started to write you letters whenever I noticed you were down. And then in high school, when you came to my room that night, I fought against myself to not take your virginity. You see, I loved you even more then, but I wanted for you to go to college and see what else was out there. Well, now you're about to graduate and I cannot hold my love in anymore. I want to make you mine. I want to kiss you, make love to you, and have you be my girlfriend. And I hope that you will still continue to enjoy my letters (I hear you talking about them to Betsy and it makes my heart soar).

Yours forever,

Fitz (aka Fitzwilliam Darcy)

P.S. I thought that you would appreciate the "Fitz" alias as you love Jane Austen books. And isn't Pride and Prejudice her best-known book? Anyway, I know that Darcy was bewitched by Elizabeth Bennett and I thought you would appreciate the reference as you have completely bewitched me forever.

P.P.S Just in case you're still unsure, it's me Nolan Montgomery.

My jaw dropped as I read the inscription and I could feel my face burning. Nolan had been Fitz? All this time. It had been him. It had been him. He loved me! It all made sense now. Why he'd been so adamant that it couldn't have been Lucas? Why I'd seen him in the post office.

Why he'd kept mentioning Jane Austen. Why he'd called me Elizabeth in bed. I laughed in giddy happiness as I realized that Nolan had loved me along. As I'd loved him. And while I was willing to accept his reasons for staying away, they made me mad. He'd wasted so much of our time! I was totally upset with him, but loved him even more for it. He'd loved me enough to walk away and wait for me. He'd been completely unselfish. He'd loved me all those years. My heart felt full and when the doorbell rang, I ran to it and jumped into his arms and kissed him.

"Why this is a welcome surprise." He grinned as he walked into the living room behind me. "I take it the date didn't go well?" he said, his expression more somber as he surveyed my face and I realized that he was jealous. I considered playing around for a few seconds but decided against it. We'd been playing games for far too long as it was.

"No, the date didn't go well, but that's not why I kissed you," I said as I grabbed his hand and pulled him toward me. "You're a doofus, you know that, right?"

"I am?" His expression was confused, and I leaned forward and gave him a quick kiss.

"I love you, Mr. Darcy," I said as I ran my hands through his hair and his expression changed to one of delight.

"You found the book."

"Yes, I found the book, Fitz." I giggled as he kissed me on the neck. "Why didn't you ever tell me?"

"I was going to tell you that weekend when I visited you in college, but you were so devastated over that guy Mark that I realized you would never love me the same way and I was just wasting my time and then you never said anything about the book..." His voice trailed off and he shrugged.

"One, I wasn't devastated over Mark. I'd been crying from

happiness because you gave me the first orgasm of my life and when you went all funny, I thought you regretted being there with me, and so I pretended I was sad over Mark and well, you know why I never mentioned the book, I didn't know until five minutes ago."

"Oh, my darling, Jules." He groaned as he pulled my dress up and off of my body. "What a silly mess."

"Yes." I laughed and then pouted. "But..."

"But what?" He frowned as he kissed along my collarbone and pulled my bra off.

"You haven't said it," I said, my words soft and slightly nervous.

"Said what?" He frowned as his fingers caressed my breasts.

"You know?" I made a face at him as he pulled his shirt off. "Nolan, is this all about sex to you?"

"What?" He stopped what he was doing and looked at me with a boyish expression. "You know this isn't about sex. I love you, Julia Gilbert. I've loved you since you were a little girl. I've loved you with all of my heart and soul. I've waited all of my life for you. It's always been you. It will always be you. You have to know that, right?"

"Okay." My voice was full of bliss. "You can continue to devour me now."

"Is that what you were waiting for?" He gave me a cocky grin. "You wanted to hear how much I loved you?"

"Yes." I smiled at him, my heart full of love.

"Well, I love you more than life itself," he said as he pulled my panties down. "I love you so much that I'm going to show you just how much." He growled as he unzipped his pants and pulled them down. He bent me forward over the couch and positioned his hardness between my legs. "I'm going to show you..." His voice trailed off as I reached behind and grabbed his cock and started stroking.

"Stop talking and just do it," I said and he growled and slid into me. I could feel his heart beating in sequence to mine as he fucked me and I'd never been so happy in my life.

"So you're going to keep going on dates?" Nolan looked pissed off as we lay in my bed in each other's arms.

"Yes, Nolan."

"But we're together now. I want to tell the world," he said as he kissed my shoulder.

"I still need to go on the dates for my job and to help the paper."

"Fine." He growled. "I'll be at all of them anyway, so they better not try any funny business."

"Oh Nolan." I laughed as he stroked my hair.

"What?" He grinned as he kissed the top of my head. "And make sure that there are no second dates, only first dates. I'm not having any of those guys feel like they're in with a chance."

"Okay, my love," I said as I kissed him softly. "I'll be the Queen of First Dates."

"Yes, you will," he said as he kissed me back. "As well as the queen of my heart."

The End

Thank you for reading Queen of First Dates, the first book in the Canyon Beach series. I really hope you enjoyed it. If you did please leave a review. I'm excited to announce that I am writing Betsy's story next and it is called, "The Kissing Bet."

To make sure you don't miss the release, please join my mailing list here! And yes, Jules and Nolan will make an appearance in the next book as well.

Here's a brief little teaser from The Kissing Bet.

I cursed the day that the Canyon Beach Lingerie shop opened. Not just because I spent money I didn't have there. And not just because I'd bought a pair of red crotchless panties that were unlike anything I'd ever seen before; they were lacy, see-through and the sexiest piece of underwear that I'd ever owned. And not just because I thought it would be a good idea to leave them on Police officer Jefferson Evian's desk when I went to the police station the day before. No, those weren't all the reasons why I cursed the day that I'd ever stepped foot inside the lingerie shop. The biggest reason was because not only had I left the "Anonymous package" on the wrong desk in the police station, but deputy sheriff, Max Fernandes had seen me leaving said package and opened it before I'd been able to slip out of the station with my empty cupcake containers.

JOIN MY MAILING LIST TO GET MORE UPDATES ON THE NEXT book and to receive a bonus scene from Nolan's point of view.

BONUS EXCERPT FROM ALONG CAME BABY

Bonus Excerpt from Along Came Baby by J. S. Cooper

It all began with two words. Two words that I never thought anyone would say to me. Especially not someone as hunky as Carter Stevens. But hey, I guess you just never know when fate is going to look you in the face and say, hey girl, tonight is your night.

"Hey, sexy." That's what he said. "Hey, *sexy*." And with that I was gone. His tone was warm, his smile was wide, his blue eyes deep, intense, sparkling as they ran up and down my body. His dark blond hair was cut low to his head, and he had a light grazing of facial hair that I wanted to caress with my fingers to see if it was soft or rough.

"Hey," I said, not knowing what else to say. I wanted to say, hey, sexy, are you as good in bed as you look, but I hadn't had that much to drink yet.

"I like that necklace," he said, his hands reaching up and lightly grazing my neck as he played with the silver necklace my mom had gotten me a few Christmases before from Tiffany's. "Oops," I said as someone hit me from behind and I stumbled forward into him. "Sorry," I said and gave him a small smile as I realized how close his lips were to mine.

"Nothing to be sorry about." He grinned as his hands reached out to my waist to steady me. The bar was packed tonight and there were people surrounding us on all sides, drinking and excited as they listened to the music and chatted. "Thanks for coming tonight, Lila." He leaned forward and whispered in my ear, his breath tickling my eardrum and making my stomach and heart skip a beat.

"No worries, thanks for inviting me," I said as coolly as I could. "This is awesome and I can't wait to see you perform. You play guitar, right?" I asked, wanting to keep the conversation going, but not knowing what else to say. I wanted to tell him to keep his hands on me. I wanted to tell him that we should find a back room somewhere so I could feel his hands all over me and his lips too. If I'd been a bit braver, I would have reached up and kissed him, but I was still feeling a bit shy. He was just so hot and he made me just a little bit nervous.

"And I sing." He nodded. "We're a local band, but we have a lot of support," he said as he looked around and nodded at some guys that were standing near us and waving.

"This is a cool spot. I've never been to Rockwood Music Hall before," I said as I looked around. The stage was directly to our left and the bar just behind us to the right. The venue was pretty small, but it was a well laid out space. I looked up and saw a balcony with seats and saw people standing and dancing to the band on the stage. Everyone seemed like they were having a lot of fun and the feeling was contagious. There was magic in the air and it seemed like everyone here knew it.

"We're going to go on in about ten minutes," he whispered into my ear again, his tongue lightly touching my inner ear. My whole body trembled at the intimacy of his action and my hands moved down to his as they were still on my waist. "I have to go to the back and grab my gear and get ready. However, let's get a drink when I'm done, yeah?" He leaned back and his eyes gazed into mine with a devilish look. The way he stared into my eyes made me think bad thoughts. Really bad thoughts.

"Just a drink?" I said, with a teasing smile, as my fingers ran down his lightly. I wasn't quite sure what had come over me. Maybe it was the two glasses of wine I'd had before I'd come out tonight. Maybe they were finally going to my head. Maybe it was the appreciative gazes he was giving me. Maybe it was the way his fingers pressed into my waist as if they wanted to get to know me better. I don't know what it was, but I was ready to have some fun tonight. No matter what that meant. And I was almost inebriated enough to let him know the thoughts in my head and exactly what I wanted.

"It's never just a drink," he said and winked and then because he knew that he was the sexiest man alive and could get away with anything, he leaned forward and gave me a quick kiss, and his hands then ran down my back to my ass and he pulled me toward him. My body was crushed against his now and he was providing me with warmth and tingles unlike any I'd felt before. "Tonight we're going to make some sweet music, baby," he said against my lips and I gasped as he slid his tongue into my mouth. He tasted like whiskey and though I've never been a huge fan of the taste before, tonight it was like manna on my lips.

"Okay," I whispered back to him as he pulled away, and I watched as he walked away toward the back of the room and through a door. I ran my hands through my hair quickly and searched in my handbag for some mints. I popped one into my mouth and sucked on it, trying to stop the flow of excitement from running through my veins. I licked my lips nervously as I stood there and walked over to the bar to get myself a drink.

There were two guys standing by the bar giving me an appreciative look and I just smiled at them coyly. In any other circumstances, I might have been interested in a little flirtation, but not tonight. Tonight, my eyes were on Carter Stevens and only Carter Stevens. He was sex on legs and I was determined to know if the promises his eyes were making would be fulfilled by the end of the night. I wasn't to know that within a month from tonight I would find out I was pregnant and the last thing I would be thinking about would be him calling me sexy.

❧ 17 ❧

I'm what some people would call a true believer. I believe in true love. The kind you read about in fairy tales. I think that somewhere out there my Prince Charming is just waiting to meet me and sweep me off of my feet. He's somewhere out there. Maybe over the rainbow. Maybe in another galaxy. Maybe he's stuck under a rock somewhere. I don't know where he is to be honest, but he sure as hell hasn't come knocking on my door in my lifetime.

Don't get me wrong I've dated some nice guys; or rather guys that seemed nice at first until I realized they weren't. I'm like a jerk magnet. The bigger the jerk, the faster they come running to me. My friends call me Lila Delilah Asshole Caller. I know it doesn't even rhyme, but I couldn't disagree with them. I think my name and phone number got put in the asshole black book or something because they love me. But I haven't given up on finding my true love. Hope springs eternal and all that good stuff. Right now, I'm just taking a little break from dating to concentrate on my career. A career I'm not really sure I'm cut out for, if I'm honest.

I work as a litigation attorney and I hate it. The only

thing I like about my job is the paycheck. Who am I to laugh at a six-figures salary? I never thought I'd make this much money in my life, and while the paychecks are great, I'd give the job up in a heartbeat if I didn't have debt up to my eyeballs. It turned out that law school was a costly endeavor and now I have to work a job I hate to pay off a debt that I got just to get the job I hate. Does that even make sense? But I digress, no one cares about my sucky job. We all have sucky jobs. I care more about finding the right man. Well, eventually. Right now, I'm just working my sucky job and swiping on dating apps hoping to get some nice dates with some nice guys. So far, I'm zero for ten. I've been on ten dates in the last six months and all the guys have been awful. I'm about ready to just say forget it and have some fun. I just don't really know who or how to have said fun. I want to get married one day. I want to have kids. I want that picture-perfect family, but I also want it with the right guy. I can picture him in my head. I've just not met him yet.

"THANK YOU SO MUCH LILA." MY NEXT-DOOR NEIGHBOR Danielle grinned at me as she handed me her spare set of keys and what looked like an expensive bottle of Pinot Noir. "You only have to look after Frosty for two nights and then my brother, Carter, will be by."

"So he'll call me to let me know when he's going to pick up the keys?" I asked as I placed her keys on my small and narrow hallway table. My apartment was very small, but had been updated, and frankly I was lucky that I could even fit in any size hallway table. I kept the bottle of wine in my hand because I was going to open that bad boy as soon as she left, right before I took her golden retriever, Frosty out for a long walk in Prospect Park.

"Yup." She nodded, her blond hair swaying back and forth as she looked at me thoughtfully. "I gave him your number and he'll call you tomorrow, I think." Her blue eyes seemed distant for a few seconds and then she smiled. "Don't worry, he will pick them up at a time available to you. He thinks he's so busy, but I told him that you're doing me a favor so he needs to pick them up at a time convenient for you."

"That's okay." I smiled at her. "He can pick them up here or at my office. So, he's going to come by in the mornings and evenings to walk Frosty?" I asked again, curiously. "I'm sorry I can't commit to taking care of him while you're away, but work is crazy right now and I'm not sure I can get away at the required hours for him to go out." I'd just started my job as an associate at a corporate law firm and the hours were awful. The pay was good, but the hours were long and tedious.

"No worries," Danielle said. "And no, I think he's going to move into my place for the next month." She made a face. "He lives on the Upper West Side, he went to Columbia and so he stayed in the area. And well it's just too much of a commute for him to go back and forth from the UWS to here." She sighed and then shuddered. "I can't imagine what my place is going to look like when I get back. He's such a slob."

"Aw, I'm sorry," I said and laughed. I knew that I had also been a slob in college as well. I was still pretty untidy now, so I was not one to judge anyone else. "That's nice that he's willing to do that for you, though."

"He's not nice at all. He's only doing it because I'm paying him." She shook her head. "Brothers!"

"Aw," I said again and then looked down at the bottle of wine in my hands. "Want some?"

"I shouldn't," she said slowly and then looked at her watch. "Okay, well maybe I have time for one glass." She stepped into my apartment properly and closed the door behind her. "Thanks, Lila."

"No worries, you brought me the wine. Come on in. I have some cheese and crackers as well. And some brownies."

"I can't have brownies." She patted her slender waist. "I just got back from yoga."

"Aw, okay." I smiled at her and sighed inwardly. I didn't want Danielle to think I was a fat ass, so I'd have to have a brownie after she left. Not that I thought she would judge me terribly, but Danielle was a new friend and I was still trying to make a good impression on her. I'd only moved into this apartment three months ago and she was my first and only friend in the building.

"But hey, who's going to tell my trainer?" She grinned as she settled down on the couch. "Plus I'm going to be in England and it's going to be freezing there. I'll need a couple of extra pounds to keep me warm at night, seeing as I won't have Frosty."

"I guess you'll miss him a lot."

"He's like my baby." She nodded. "But he'll have a lot of fun with Carter. Carter loves to jog so I'm sure Carter will be out all the time."

"That will be good for Frosty," I said with a smile as I opened the bottle of wine. Young college guys were so lucky to have so much time to go jogging. I rarely had any time to do anything now that I was working full time as an associate at a law firm. I'd always wanted to be a lawyer, and I enjoyed my job, for the most part, but I just had to work so damn much. If it wasn't for the very nice pay, I think I definitely would have pursued a different career.

"Yeah, Frosty loves Carter, but then everyone loves Carter." She rolls her eyes. "To say he's a ladies' man is an understatement."

"Oh?" I asked curiously, wondering what her brother looked like.

"Yeah." She took the glass of wine that I handed her. "You know there are some men that can say and do anything and get away with it because they're so good looking and charming?"

"Not personally, but I know the type you mean." I laughed, and we clinked glasses. "Cheers."

"Cheers," she said, and she took a small sip. "My parents even fall under his spell, he can do no wrong."

"Aw," I said again, not really knowing what to say. She wasn't exactly painting her brother in the best light.

"Oh, don't get me wrong." She shook her head and laughed as she sipped some more wine. "I love him. He's an amazing brother. Lots of fun and he's always been here for me." She nodded. "I think I'm just a little bitter because guys seem to just get away with so much."

"I understand, girl, don't worry." I pat her on the shoulder. Danielle and her boyfriend had recently broken up and while they hadn't dated for a tremendously long time, she was still upset. I was pretty sure he had cheated on her or something like that, but she hadn't told me too much.

"And I can't believe the office is sending me to England for this project." She rolled her eyes. "Like I was the only one they could think of." She shook her head again. Danielle worked in HR for some hotel chain, and supposedly they needed her to go and help with the staffing for some new hotel chain they'd acquired because half of the staff had quit in the last week.

"I think because we're single women, we're the first ones that are chosen for the not so nice jobs," I said thinking about my own experience at the law firm I worked at. I was on the most boring cases with the most discovery and the longest hours, but I accepted it as paying my dues. "When you get back, we will go and have a fun night out."

"That would be amazing." Danielle's blue eyes lit. "Have I told you how happy I am that you moved in here?"

"Only like a hundred times, so please keep it up." I grinned at her. "And you're not half as happy as I am," I said honestly. Moving into this apartment three months ago had been like a dream come true. I'd finally been able to afford my own place and even though I was decorating it slowly, it was really starting to feel like a home. "I got really lucky moving into this gorgeous place and getting an awesome new neighbor and a friend to boot."

"Aw, you're so sweet, Lila," Danielle said. "Here's to us," she said and raised her glass again.

"Also." She paused, her face looking slightly awkward and nervous for some reason as she looked at me.

"Yeah?" I prodded for her to continue, curious as what she was going to say next.

"So I shouldn't say this and I normally wouldn't but . . ." Her voice trailed off again, and she just shook her head. "My brother, Carter, he's a very charismatic, very good-looking guy and, well, he's a lot of fun, but he's a total playboy."

"Okay?" I laughed. "Why are you telling me this?"

"You're a pretty girl, Lila," she said with a smile. "My brother loves pretty girls. And he loves the chase, so he's going to want you badly. I'm sure of it. Don't give him the time of day. He's a heartbreaker, pure and simple."

"I'll remember that." I grinned at her. "I'm not looking for a relationship or anything right now, so I think we're good."

"I know you've said that before but I figured I'd give you my advanced warning, just in case."

"Thanks, but no need to worry about me. Between work and sleep I have no time for anything else. I'm a regular boring Betty."

"I don't think you're a boring Betty, but just remember what I said. He can be a real charmer when he wants to be and well, I've seen too many friends fall under his spell and then . . ." Her voice trailed off and she made a face. "But let's have one more glass of wine before I have to go. It's going to be a long flight tonight."

"You'll have a great time," I said as I poured her some more wine. "And don't worry about Frosty. I'll make sure to remind Carter to walk him if I see him around the building."

"Thanks, Lila. You're amazing," she said as we clinked glasses one more time and we both took another long sip of the expensive wine she'd brought me.

"Also, you don't have to worry about me, I'm not into college guys." I laughed. "I'm way too old to hang."

"College?" She looked at me with a confused expression. "Oh, he's not in college." She laughed. "Though you'd think he only recently graduated. He's actually slightly older than me. He's thirty-five."

"Oh," I said. "I thought he was a lot younger than that from the way you were talking about him. I'm surprised I've never met him before. He's not come over before?"

"No." She shook her head. "He's a busy guy. He works on Wall Street during the day and he's in some stupid band that plays a lot of local gigs." She rolled her eyes. "He thinks he's some sort of rock god."

"Oh yeah?" I asked curiosity getting the better of me. I loved musicians for some reason. They were just so talented and sexy. Though I wasn't going to tell Danielle that; I'd always imagined having some sort of secret fling with a rock star. I didn't want her to start worrying about me.

"Yeah." She finished up her wine. "We usually get together for lunches during the week because his nights and weekends are packed. I should feel honored he made time to look after Frosty."

"If he's a Wall Street banker, why are you paying him?" I asked as I just remembered what she'd said earlier.

"Because he's the devil." She laughed and stood up. "Okay, I should get going. Thanks once again, Lila. I'll see you in a month." And with that she hurried out of my apartment so she could hurry to the airport and hopefully not miss her flight.

"Bye, Danielle," I called after her as I sat back and continued to sip on my wine. I tried to imagine what her brother looked like, but then laughed at myself. I was horribly busy with work right now and it seemed as if he was really busy as well, so I'm sure it's unlikely that we would see each other at all asides from when he picked up the keys. I grabbed the remote control and turned the TV on to try to find a cooking show before I got up to take Frosty on his evening walk.

"OH COME ON," I SAID TAPPING MY FOOT AGAINST THE wooden floor as I waited for my doorbell to ring. "Where are you, Carter?" I muttered under my breath as I stared at my watch. Five more minutes had passed, and he still wasn't here. I was going to miss the next train which meant I was going to miss my connecting train, which meant I was going to be late for work. I walked back to the living room from the hallway and sat on the couch, trying not to look at my watch again. I grabbed my phone and scrolled to my text messages. He'd said he would be here at 8:30 a.m. to get the keys. Had I somehow read it wrong? Did he mean 8:30 p.m.? It was now 9:00 a.m. How could he say 8:30 a.m. and be this late? He had to know I had to work. I typed into the phone and sent him another text message.

"Hey, Carter, it's me, Lila, just checking you're still coming this

morning? :)" I added a smiley face, so he wouldn't know how annoyed I was, just in case my text message read as passive aggressive.

"*Yup.*" He text back. I waited to see if he was going to say more than that. Like a *sorry, I'm late*, or *the trains are delayed* or something. But nope, all he said was "yup" like he wasn't already thirty minutes behind.

"*Do you have an ETA?*" I typed finally as I realized another five minutes had passed and still nothing. I watched the screen intensely as I saw the three dots appear to show me that he was typing a response, but then they stopped. They stopped and no message came. "Are you frigging joking me?" I hissed at the screen. How could he start typing a response and then just not respond, knowing he was already late. Why wouldn't he just tell me he was running late? He had absolutely no respect for my time. No respect at all. I knew he was busy as well, but come on now. He was the one that had texted me to say that this morning would be best for him to get the keys as had some gig tonight and didn't know when he'd be around. I wondered to myself if he was really going to be able to take care of Frosty properly, but he knew what he was doing. It was his sister's dog after all, he would have to make the time. I gnawed on my lower lip as I realized another ten minutes had passed and still not a word from Carter. He was starting to really piss me off now. Did he have no respect for my time at all?

"*Hey are you going to be here soon?*" I sent another text message. And I didn't add a smiley face this time. I didn't care that he hadn't responded as yet. No one could call me psycho for constantly texting in a situation like this.

"Yup," he responded immediately, and I screamed. Yup? What the hell did yup mean? I was normally an even-keeled person, but this morning was already off to a rough start. Frosty had gone potty on Danielle's rug so I'd had to clean that up before I took him on his walk and then he had been so busy trying to chase every squirrel that he saw that he didn't want to go potty for ages. I'd had to take a five-minute shower, had nicked myself while shaving and then to make matters worse, my favorite black blazer had felt too tight when I'd put it on, so I'd had to wear my gray suit instead. And I hated my gray suit.

"How long will you be? I have to get to work and now I'm already running late." I typed out again. Let him feel bad for being tardy. I didn't care if he was some hot shot banker and musician, he needed to respect other people's time.

Ding Dong. The doorbell rang as soon as I pressed send, but I didn't feel guilty. "Finally," I mumbled as I jumped up off of the couch and hurried to the front door and pulled it open hastily. "You made it," I muttered before even making eye contact with him.

"Hi there, Lila, right? I'm Carter. Sorry for the delay. The line in the coffee shop was way too long, and I wanted to get you a latte and bagel with lox and cream cheese. Danielle told me they were your favorites." The man in front of me gave me an easy, lazy smile, his blue eyes were open and friendly and his perfect white teeth gleamed at me.

"Hi." That was all I managed to squeak out as I stared at Carter. Danielle had understated just how good-looking her brother was. He wasn't just good-looking. He was gorgeous. Absolutely gorgeous. He stood at about six-four with a solid muscular build. He had dark golden blond hair that surrounded his face perfectly. His blue eyes were azure in color and reminded me of the ocean colors I'd seen in the Caribbean.

"Here you go," he said, and he handed me a small cup from my favorite coffee shop and a brown bag with a still warm bagel inside. "I hope that they are as good as you remember them being."

"Thanks," I said as I took the cup and bag from him. I gave him a huge smile, all my anger having faded away as soon as I'd seen his smile. "Would you like to come inside?"

"Willing to share some of that bagel?" He grinned and gave me a small wink as he walked into my apartment. He made my hallway feel like it was a part of a doll's house and my heart raced as I stood next to him and stared at his muscles up close and personal. "I forgot to get one for myself."

"Oh, of course." I grinned at him. "Come on in," I said and waved him to follow me down the hallway to the kitchen.

"Should I take my shoes off?" he asked as he paused next to the door. He was wearing a white T-shirt that said, *No Sleep Till Brooklyn*, and blue faded jeans that clung to his hips.

"No, that's okay." I swallowed hard to stop myself from telling him that he could take his T-shirt off if he wanted. I didn't know what had come over me. I couldn't stop looking at his biceps and imagine his big hands all over me. I reddened as I realized that I was totally fantasizing over him and I'd just met him.

"Okay, are you sure you have time for the bagel?" He gave me a boyish grin as I took two plates out of the cupboard. "You said you were running late in your text, right?"

"I'm already late." I wrinkled my nose at him as I grabbed a knife to cut the bagel in half. "What's thirty more minutes going to do?"

"You'll have to let me get you an Uber into your job," he said as he took the plate from me and grabbed the bagel. "Mmm," He made a noise as he took a bite and chewed. "This is delicious."

"Glad you approve," I said and took a bite myself. The bagel was toasted perfectly and had just the right amount of cream cheese and lox. "Yummy," I said as I swallowed. I placed the plate on the table and then opened the fridge door. "Would you like some orange juice?"

"Yes, please," he said, and he walked over to the fridge and stood next to me. "Thanks for your hospitality by the way." He ran his hand through his hair and smiled at me. "Danielle told me you were nice and I guess she was right."

"She's great." I smiled back at him, ignoring the urge to pat my hair to make sure that it was in place. "I'm so glad that she's my neighbor."

"You just moved in recently, right?" he said as he took the glass of orange juice. His blue eyes gazed into mine as if he were genuinely interested in the answer.

"Yes." I nodded. "I just moved to New York about two years ago. I started working at this firm about six months ago and moved in here three months ago."

"You're a lawyer, right?"

"Yes. I went to law school at the University of Iowa."

"Go Hawkeyes," he said, and I looked at him in surprise. "I might not look like it, but I'm a huge fan of college football."

"Oh?"

"Yeah, my family is from Ohio so we're Ohio State fans, but I can respect the Iowa team, though they're not as good as the Buckeyes."

"You wish." I laughed. Carter Stevens was the last person I would have assumed to have been into college football. He just looked too cool and sexy to be into something so every day.

"So you came here after law school? And started working for the firm?"

"I moved here and worked for a non-profit, but then upgraded to a firm." I made a face. "More money and all that jazz."

"I see." He nodded. "And you're single?"

"Maybe," I said coyly, surprised by his question. "Why do you ask?" I bit down on my lower lip and gazed at him as he finished eating his bagel.

"Because I'd be devastated to find out you had a boyfriend."

"Danielle was right." I laughed. "You really are a huge flirt, aren't you?"

"I'm not a flirt." He shook his head. "Well, not with everyone."

"I'm one of the lucky ones, am I?"

"Of course, you're a very lucky one." He winked at me and then before I could blink he was reaching over and lightly removing a random piece of bagel from the side of my mouth. I watched as he popped it inside of his. "Didn't want to waste any of it now."

"You." I was speechless. Had he really just eaten a crumb from the side of my mouth?

"Yes, what about me?"

"I, I just don't know what to say." I shook my head at him. It was weird to know that we'd just met. A part of me felt so comfortable with him; as if I'd known him for years.

"You have beautiful brown eyes," he stated then and within seconds he was singing "Brown Eyed Girl" by Van Morrison; one of my absolute favorite songs. "Do you remember when we used to sing . . ." His voice was deep and smooth and I joined him in the chorus, even though my voice sounded like something from the reject episodes of *American Idol*. My voice trailed off as he continued singing as I didn't know all the words and I just stood there sipping my coffee watching this absolutely gorgeous man sing to me. It was surreal, it was ridiculous, and I absolutely loved it. Things like this just didn't happen to me. And while a part of me was extremely ill-at-ease and slightly embarrassed, there was just something about Carter that made his being so over-the-top seem quite normal.

"So, brown-eyed girl, what are you doing tonight?"

"Tonight?" I stared at him wondering where he was going with this conversation. Could he also be into me?

"Yeah tonight." He grinned. "I have a gig at Rockwood Music Hall, maybe you'd like to come?"

"Um, well, I work," I stammered.

"You're telling me you have to work all night?"

"No, I'm just saying that I'm already late for work and I have a lot of files to go through today. We're going to trial next week, and well, I just don't know when I'll be free."

"Make yourself free." He gave me an impish grin. "I'll make it worth your while."

"Oh yeah?" I asked, loving the way he was so easy and teasing with me. "You don't even know me."

"Well, I know where you live." His phone beeped then, and he grabbed it from his pocket. I watched as he made a face. "But that's my cue to go and check on Frosty. I need to change and head off to work myself."

"Aw, okay," I said, feeling disappointed, but knowing it was for the best. I could talk to Carter Stevens all day and night. "I was wondering what investment firm you worked for that you could wear jeans and a T-shirt."

"Hey, that's how we do it on Wall Street these days." He laughed and then his face grew slightly serious. "But I really should be going now. Thanks for the keys. And for looking after Frosty for a couple of days. I hope you can make it tonight, the show is at eight. If not, I guess I'll see you around this place."

"Yeah, I guess so," I said, suddenly feeling sad. What if I never really saw him? I mean, I didn't see Danielle all that often. He was hot and sexy and he was flirting with me and I liked it. Granted he most probably wasn't going to be the love of my life, but he could be the fun of my life. I needed some fun. He seemed like the perfect guy to have some fun with. I was going to go to that show tonight even if it meant I had to go back to the office afterward. I knew it would be worth it.

You can purchase and read "Along Came Baby" here.

42933609R00113

Printed in Poland
by Amazon Fulfillment
Poland Sp. z o.o., Wrocław